Like a
BROKEN Doll

ANNE   APF

SADDLEBACK
EDUCATIONAL PUBLISHING

URBAN UNDERGROUND

SADDLEBACK
EDUCATIONAL PUBLISHING
www.sdlback.com

© 2011 by Saddleback Educational Publishing

ISBN-13: 978-1-61651-005-3
ISBN-10: 1-61651-005-6
eBook: 978-1-60291-790-3

Printed in Guangzhou, China
0510/05-72-10

15 14 13 12 11   1 2 3 4 5

CHAPTER ONE

"My purse!" a girl standing in front of Harriet Tubman's statue at Tubman High School screamed. "There's a hundred dollars missing from my purse!"

About a dozen kids were arriving for Monday's classes when she began yelling. One of them was Jaris Spain. He knew the girl—Ryann Kern—but he didn't know her well. She was in his American History I class. All he knew about her was that she was very smart, and she was a loner with one friend, Leticia Hicks.

Now Leticia grabbed Ryann's hand and cried, "Oh my gosh! Are you sure, Ryann? Are you sure it's gone?"

"It's not here," Ryann screamed. She dropped to her knees at the foot of the statue and dumped out the contents of her purse. Lipsticks, mirrors, papers, a driver's license all flew out. She groped through the mess frantically, crying, "It's not here! It's gone! It was in my wallet. I put it in my wallet and now it's gone!"

Jaris drew closer. Some of his friends were near Ryann, looking at her sympathetically. Sereeta Prince was there. So were Alonee Lennox and Sami Archer.

"Girl, could you have dropped it on the bus?" Sami asked. "If you did, they got a special number you can call. The bus driver hangs on to stuff like that."

"No!" Ryann cried. "I had it a few minutes ago. I leaned my purse against the base of the statue, and I turned my head to talk to somebody. Somebody must've reached in and grabbed the money." Ryann began to glare at the girls closest to her. She took an especially hard look at Sereeta. "Did you see anybody near my purse?" Ryann asked her, "You were right here, Sereeta."

"No," Sereeta responded, "I didn't see anything."

"A hundred dollars!" Ryann moaned, beginning to cry. "Mom gave it to me this morning. I was going to go shopping at Lawson's for my summer clothes. I was going to get all the cute tank tops and shorts on sale. I can't believe somebody reached in my purse and stole my money!"

"Nobody here would have done that," Jaris said. He knew all the kids who were near enough to Ryann to have been able to reach her purse. "There's gotta be some mistake."

"I'm going to report it to the office," Ryann cried. "I'm going to let them know there's a thief here who has my hundred dollars!"

Jaris glanced at Sereeta. She looked very upset. She leaned close to Jaris and said, "She thinks I took it. I was the closest

3

to the purse of anybody, and I think she suspects me! I feel so horrible."

"Don't worry about it," Jaris consoled her. "Everybody who knows you knows you wouldn't do something like that."

Slowly, the students dispersed to their first classes. Even before this happened, Jaris had been worried about Sereeta. She was going through a lot lately. Her mother and stepfather had had their first child. They had been paying little attention to Sereeta in their excitement over the new baby. Sereeta felt lonely and abandoned. Now she seemed badly shaken.

Jaris tried to remember all the students he saw near Ryann. Alonee and Sami were there, but he was willing to bet his life on their honesty. Jasmine, Marko Lane's girl-friend, was there too. Marko lavished gifts on her, but she always wanted more. She was mean and sly. She might have ripped off the hundred dollars.

Then there was another guy, new to Tubman High. Quincy Pierce seemed nice enough, but Jaris didn't know him yet. Maybe his family was tight on money. Maybe he was hurting for cash. Could Ryann have been careless enough to leave her purse open when she put it down? Did Quincy—or someone else—see a hundred dollar bill sticking out of her wallet and just grab the bill on impulse?

Jasmine was still hanging around the statue of Harriet Tubman after the others had left. "Too bad about Ryann losing her money like that, huh Jasmine?" Jaris asked.

Jasmine shrugged. "Stupid chick," she replied. "She stacks her purse against the statue and then looks the other way. She asked for it. She got what was coming to her. You gotta keep your purse with you all the time. Ryann, she thinks she's so smart 'cause she gets As, but she's got no common sense."

Jaris looked at Jasmine, hoping he could read some sign of guilt in her face, but she was cool. Even if she had taken the

money, she'd never show any emotion.
"Seems terrible we can't even trust the kids
we go to school with," Jaris commented.

"I'll tell you who I don't trust, boy. That
girl you hang around with—Sereeta."
There was a sneer on Jasmine's face. "She
is one sick puppy."

"What's that supposed to mean?" Jaris
snapped.

"She always cryin'," Jasmine complained. "What's that about, huh? Maybe
she got mental problems. You ever hear of
people who steal 'cause they're sick in the
head?"

"Sereeta is fine," Jaris insisted. "She
doesn't have any mental problems."

"Well, all I know is," Jasmine asserted,
"nobody's gonna take what's in this girl's
purse. They even try, I'll scratch them
bloody."

As Jaris walked to his class, he wasn't
sure what to think. Jasmine's father had a
good job in banking. The family wasn't
hurting for money. Jasmine didn't need to

6

steal another girl's hundred dollars unless she saw the chance and took it just for spite.

Later in the school day, Quincy joined Jaris, Alonee, and Sami for lunch. Sereeta was usually there too, but she went home from school early. She said she wasn't feeling well, and that worried Jaris even more. Maybe the accusation that she took the money had gotten to her, adding to the stresses she already had.

"Too bad Ryann lost her hundred dollars," Jaris said to Quincy, wondering how he'd react.

"Yeah man," Quincy responded, "if I lost a hundred dollars, my mom would freak big time. I'd be afraid to go home. Mom does housekeeping at the hospital, and she doesn't make much money. My dad's sick. So a hundred bucks is big stuff for us."

"It's a tough break for Ryann," Sami chimed in. "I feel for the girl."

"I just can't imagine somebody being nervy enough to reach into some girl's purse when she's only a few feet away," Alonee commented. "I mean, Ryann turns her back for a minute, and somebody darts over and grabs it? I gotta believe the money just fell out of her purse earlier, and she wants to believe it was stolen."

"You know what I heard that witch Leticia say?" Sami asked. "I heard her say she's pretty sure Sereeta took the money. That burned me good. I go, 'Where you get off accusing another girl you don't even know, sister?' And she goes, 'She was right there, and I don't like her anyway.'"

Jaris was saddened to hear Sami say that. It added to his worries about Sereeta. He needed to talk to Ryann and Leticia and convince them that Sereeta was a good and honest person. If they really knew her, they would never call her a thief.

After school that day, when Ryann and Leticia came walking toward the bus stop, Jaris stepped into their path. "Hi," he said in a friendly voice. "The money turn up yet?"

"Are you kidding?" Leticia snapped. "The dirty thief who took it is out spending it and having fun!"

Ryann dabbed at her eyes as if she had been crying. "This is the meanest thing anybody ever did to me," she moaned. "I had all my stuff picked out at Lawson's. Now I got to ask my parents for another hundred dollars."

"Ryann," Jaris told her, "I just want you to know that Sereeta didn't take your money. I've known her all my life, and she's a really honest person. She'd never steal from anybody."

Leticia was a tall, plain girl. She wore her hair severely pulled back. She looked like she didn't trust many people, and she looked older than her age of sixteen. "She's your girlfriend so you'd stick with her," Leticia replied. "All I know is she was right there next to Ryann's purse. When I looked at her, she had this guilty expression on her face. I'm pretty good at reading the looks on peoples' faces."

Ryann took out her handkerchief and wiped her eyes. "It's just so m-mean to steal from somebody," she sobbed.

"If she's your girlfriend," Leticia said to Jaris, "tell her to give the money back."

"Look, she didn't take it," Jaris snapped.

"The bus is coming," Leticia said. "Come on, Ryann."

Jaris felt sick. Sereeta was one of the most beautiful girls at Tubman High School. She had glossy black curls, honey-colored skin, and sparkling eyes. A lot of girls at Tubman envied Sereeta because she was so beautiful. Boys looked at her when she passed by and the other girls noticed her. Jaris had loved Sereeta since they were both in middle school. It broke his heart to see her accused of stealing. But how could he prove she was innocent? Neither Ryann nor Leticia was very attractive, and it was easy for them to believe bad things about Sereeta.

After the girls got on the bus, Jaris wanted to make sure Sereeta was all right and texted her: "R U OK." He waited a while for her reply but none came. So he rode his motorcycle over to her house. When he rang the doorbell, Sereeta's mother, Olivia, came. She was holding her newborn son, Jake. "Hi," she said in a girlish voice. "Wassup?" She was in her midthirties, but she acted much younger.

"Sereeta left school early. She said she wasn't feeling well. I just wanted to make sure she was okay," Jaris explained. "If she is, maybe I could say hi to her."

"I don't think she came home," Sereeta's mother replied. "I haven't seen her. She should be coming home soon I suppose."

"Uh, you mean she didn't come home around one?" Jaris asked.

The baby started to cry, and the woman jiggled him on her hip. "There, there, Jake. . . . No, I haven't seen Sereeta all day. I don't see much of her. She's got a lot going on in her life. Clubs or something," she said.

"Well, when she gets home, will you ask her to call Jaris?" Jaris asked.

"I will," the woman said. "I think she's doing a play at school or something."

"She was in a play quite a while ago," Jaris replied. "But that's over."

"Oh," Olivia Manley said. "Then it couldn't be that."

Back on the street, Jaris tried Sereeta's cell phone again, but he was transferred to voice mail. It was getting late in the day, and he was getting more worried. Jaris headed home, but he kept calling Sereeta with no luck.

When Jaris got home, he told his mother what had happened at school. "This girl kinda blamed Sereeta as if she stole her hundred dollars. I think it really got to Sereeta and she left school early, but I don't know where she is."

Jaris's mother frowned. "Did you call her mom?" she asked.

"Yeah, I went over there," Jaris answered, "but she didn't seem to be worried or to know where Sereeta was." Jaris tried calling Olivia Manley again. Surely Sereeta was home by now.

The phone rang for a long time before a man answered. "Perry Manley here," Sereeta's stepfather announced.

"Hi, I'm Jaris Spain, a friend of Sereeta's. Is she home?" Jaris inquired.

"Uh," he hesitated. Jaris heard him yelling. "Is Sereeta home, Olivia?" Then he returned to the phone and told Jaris, "No, she's not home."

"Do you know where she is?" Jaris asked impatiently. "What was *wrong* with these people?" he thought. It was getting dark.

"She's a teenager," Manley laughed. "Who knows where they are most of the time?"

"Yeah," Jaris replied. "But it's getting late, and she left school around one, and now it's after six-thirty. Aren't you guys a little worried?"

"Oh, she's probably hanging out with her friends," Manley suggested in a casual voice. "She's got a lot of friends. When she gets in, I'll tell her you called. Who did you say you were again?"

"Jaris Spain," Jaris snapped, almost hanging up the receiver in the man's ear.

Jaris's little sister, Chelsea, came to the doorway of his room. She was fourteen years old. "Wassup?" she asked.

"I'm worried about Sereeta, chili pepper," Jaris explained. "Some creeps at school accused her of stealing some money, and it really freaked her out. She felt so bad she left school early, and now I don't know where she is."

Chelsea flopped down on a chair in Jaris's room. "One time in sixth grade," she told Jaris, "some dumb girl said I stole her necklace. It was just a cheap thing, but she thought it was great. She accused me of stealing it. She told everybody I stole it, and I didn't. Then she found it in the bathroom where it fell behind the toilet."

Jaris agreed with his little sister. "I think maybe this girl at school just lost her hundred dollars too, and she thinks somebody stole it. But Sereeta was so upset she just took off." He shook his head. "I don't know where she is."

"I've seen her sitting on those old stones in the field sometimes," Chelsea offered.

"What?" Jaris asked, jerking to attention. "What are you talking about?"

Chelsea shrugged. "Me and my friends were riding bikes," Chelsea explained, "and we saw her sitting there one time. You know the little pizza place over behind Iroquois Street? Well, there's a field about a block away where there's a house that burned down. There's pepper trees and the foundation of the old house that burned. Anyways, sometimes she sits there."

"Wow!" Jaris exclaimed.

"We didn't want to bother her because she was sorta crying," Chelsea added.

"Thanks, chili pepper," Jaris said as he ran outside and jumped on his motorcycle. He was soon moving through the darkness to Iroquois Street. Before he got there, he again called Sereeta's cell, but he got no answer.

When Jaris got to the place Chelsea described, he saw Sereeta sitting on part of the stone foundation.

"Sereeta!" he shouted as he rode up. He stopped the motorcycle and got off. "What're you doing here? It's past seven o'clock."

"Oh Jaris, I just came here to think," Sereeta answered. "I was thinking about stuff, and I sort of leaned on one of the stones and fell asleep."

"I tried a million times to call you on your cell, Sereeta," Jaris told her. "I was really worried."

"I'm sorry I worried you, Jaris," she said.

"Sereeta, you need to go home now," Jaris insisted.

"Are they worried about me? My mother and my stepfather?" she asked with a half smile on her lips. There was a deep bitterness in her eyes.

Jaris wondered if she did this to try to alarm her mother, to arouse some stirring of motherly instinct. If Sereeta hoped for such a reaction, she didn't get it.

"Climb on behind me, Sereeta," Jaris told her, mounting the motorcycle. "I'll have you home in no time."

As they pulled out and onto the street, Sereeta held on tightly to Jaris. "I didn't know you had a motorcycle, Jaris," she shouted over the noise of the bike.

"My dad just gave it to me. He fixed up an old one from the shop and asked me if I'd like it. I said, 'Pop, are you kidding?'" Jaris explained.

"Thanks for coming to get me, Jaris," Sereeta said. "Did you hear any more about the stolen money?"

"No, most of us think she just dropped it somewhere and thinks it was stolen," Jaris replied. "She'll find it on the floor of her room or somewhere."

After a few moments, Sereeta said, "They all died in that house, you know."

"What?" Jaris shouted back to her.

"Where the foundation stones are," Sereeta explained. "The people who lived there died in the fire. When the house burned down, you know. It's so peaceful there. I can feel their spirits. I think they were suffering a lot before the fire for some reason. Then they left this earth and found peace. I think when you're near the spirits of the dead who were happy to be leaving this earth, you can feel their serenity. It's a good thing."

Jaris felt scared. He felt more scared than he had in a long time, or maybe ever.

CHAPTER TWO

Jaris pulled into the driveway of the Manley house and shut off the motorcycle. Then he turned and took hold of Sereeta's arm before she got off the bike. "Sereeta, don't worry about that girl's missing money. Don't let it get to you. Anybody who knows you knows you wouldn't take a dime that wasn't yours." He helped Sereeta off, and then he kissed her. "I love you babe," he whispered to her. "I love you so much that it makes me freakin' crazy when you're hurting."

Just then, angry voices floated from the Manley house. Sereeta stiffened at the sound.

Perry Manley was shouting. "It's just that I'd like to think I still have a wife to come home to, that you're not in that nursery fussing over the baby twenty-four-seven,"

"I can't believe you're jealous of your own son," Olivia Manley cried. "Perry, I need to be a mother to our baby!"

"We need to get a nanny, Olivia," Perry demanded. "You're over the top with this baby deal. There's no balance. We can't even sit down to dinner together. I feel like I'm a single guy again, eating by myself."

Sereeta closed her eyes for a moment. She seemed embarrassed. She turned and hurried toward the door. She paused there and waved to Jaris. Then she rushed inside.

Jaris headed home, even more worried about Sereeta. It sounded as if her mother's new marriage had run into stormy waters already. And Sereeta had been through so much already. When she was in middle school her parents divorced, sending

CHAPTER TWO

her into a deep depression. Then her mother remarried, and she and her new husband were so excited about the baby on the way that Sereeta seemed to cease to exist for them. Now there was even more trouble.

When Jaris got home, Chelsea was in the front yard waiting for him. "Hi Jare. Was she there where I said?" she asked.

"Yeah, chili pepper, I really appreciate that tip you gave me," Jaris answered, jumping off his motorcycle and putting it into the garage. Then he came over and kissed Chelsea on the top of her head, in the middle of her reddish brown curls. "I owe you, little sister. I found Sereeta just sitting there in a daze. I took her home."

"Were her parents glad to see her?" Chelsea asked.

"No, they were having a fight," Jaris said.

"If we hung out late like that, Mom would be worried sick," Chelsea commented. "Pop too."

21

"Yeah. We got good parents, chili pepper. You know, I think Sereeta is in big trouble. She's like a boat without a rudder, and I don't know what to do about it."

Chelsea looked down at her jeans, rubbing at a spot on her knee. She seemed to be struggling with herself about something. Finally she looked up at Jaris and told him, "I promised her I'd never tell, but maybe I should."

"Who did you promise not to tell?" Jaris asked.

"Sereeta," the little sister responded. "I promised her I wouldn't tell anybody, but . . ." Chelsea's brow was furrowed. "But maybe somebody needs to know."

Jaris took his sister's hand and led her over to the little stone bench in the garden. They both sat down. "Chelsea," Jaris said fervently, "you know I care about Sereeta probably more than anybody else in this world does. Her parents just seem so busy with their own stuff that they don't care.

I think Sereeta needs a friend now more than ever, so I need to know what's going on with her, okay?"

Chelsea's eyes widened. She grasped the seriousness in her brother's voice. "Okay," she began, "when me and Jacklyn were biking and we saw her in that field. We saw her before she saw us and . . . she was . . . hurting herself."

Jaris turned cold. "What do you mean?"

"She had this knife . . . she cut her arm," Chelsea explained. "She did it a couple of times. They weren't big cuts, I mean like gashes or something, but her arm was bleeding. It was really gross. . . . And then she saw us and she quick pulled down her sweater sleeves."

Jaris felt shaky inside, but he kept his voice calm so that Chelsea wouldn't be scared into thinking she said too much. Jaris had heard about psychologically disturbed girls and young women who cut themselves on purpose. The hurt of the cuts seemed to ease the pain they felt in their minds. "Are you sure that's what she was doing, Chelsea?" Jaris asked.

"Yeah, because you know Jacklyn," Chelsea asserted. "She's real bold, and she gets off her bike and goes up to Sereeta and says, 'Hey, watcha doin', girl? Don't it hurt when you cut yourself like that?'"

"What did Sereeta say?" Jaris asked.

"She acted like she was scared we saw her doing that," Chelsea said. "She looked at me and goes, 'Don't tell Jaris, okay? He wouldn't understand. He'd get all freaked.' I told her I wouldn't tell. Jacklyn did too. Sereeta said she never did it before. She said she just wanted to see what it felt like. She said she saw on the Internet about people doing it and it helped them, and she thought maybe it'd help her too."

"Thanks for telling me, Chelsea," Jaris said. "You did the right thing."

"You won't tell her that I told you, will you?" Chelsea pleaded. "I like Sereeta. When I was having trouble with math in fifth grade, she came and tutored me. Remember, Jare?

She helped me a lot. I think I woulda flunked if she hadn't helped me. I'd hate for her to know I didn't keep my promise not to tell."

"Some promises can't be kept," Jaris assured her. "I swear to you, though, that she'll never know you told me. You did a brave thing telling me, chili pepper. When somebody you care about is in trouble, the people who love that person need to know the truth."

Chelsea went back to her room, but Jaris sat on the bench for a few minutes. Sereeta was in even deeper trouble than Jaris had feared. He wanted desperately to help her, but he didn't know how. Jaris remembered a song he heard last year at a rap rock concert. It reminded him of Sereeta now.

> Like a broken doll,
> She came apart in my hands,
> Until I couldn't find the pieces
>   anymore,
> In the pieces of my broken heart.

The next day, Tuesday, was very warm. At school, Jaris noticed that Sereeta had been wearing long-sleeved sweatshirts and hoodies, but the weather had been cloudy and cool. Now the clouds lifted and a hot sun beat down on the Tubman campus. And Sereeta was still wearing long sleeves.

Alonee ran into Sereeta before Jaris did. "Girl, what's with the long sleeves?" she asked, laughing. "I'm cooking in a T-shirt!"

"Oh, the school rooms are air-conditioned," Sereeta explained, "and they can get cold."

"But aren't you too warm now?" Alonee insisted.

"I'm fine," Sereeta said.

Jaris walked over to Sereeta. "How's it going?" he asked her.

Sereeta shrugged. "I'm sorry you had to hear all that last night," Sereeta apologized. "They're arguing more and more. Mom always said that having the baby would bring them together, but it's tearing them apart. Mom wants to dote on Jake all the time. Now she can't go partying with my stepfather like he wants. I'm not sure where Mom is coming from. I heard her tell some friends on the phone that she doesn't think she loves the baby as much as she should. She was wondering if there was something wrong with her. I think she's spending so much time with the baby just to prove to herself that she loves him enough."

"They'll probably work it out," Jaris assured her. Jaris couldn't help staring at Sereeta's long sleeves. The cuts probably had not healed yet. "Sereeta, I know you've been under a lot of pressure . . . if you ever want to just talk about something, I'd be glad to listen, you know. If it'd help . . ."

"Yeah, okay," Sereeta said, then changed the subject. "Heard anything more about that missing money? She didn't find it, did she? I was so hoping she'd find it under the bed or something."

"I haven't heard anything," Jaris said.

Midmorning, in Mr. Goodman's math class, there was a major commotion before the teacher came in. Alonee, Sereeta, and

Jasmine were already seated while other students were walking up to the teacher's desk to drop off their math homework. Marko and Leticia Hicks had just finished adding their homework to the pile when a junior—Liza Ann Wallace—screamed, "Where's my wallet?" She leaped to her feet. "I just turned in my homework and my wallet was in my purse right here! Now it's gone!"

Jasmine glanced over at Sereeta who sat just behind Liza Ann. "Okay Sereeta," Jasmine demanded, "give the girl back her wallet. This gig is getting old, girl."

"Are you crazy?" Sereeta cried. "I didn't touch her purse!"

"Look, Liza Ann," Alonee said, "your wallet is lying there under your desk. It must have slipped from your purse when you got up."

Liza Ann stooped and picked up the wallet. "Look! It's empty! I had twenty-five dollars in that wallet this morning and now it's gone."

Leticia was sitting alongside Sereeta. All eyes turned to her. "Leticia," Liza Ann asked, "did you see anybody at my purse?"

"I'm sorry," Leticia answered, "I wasn't looking. I was going over today's assignment."

Mr. Goodman came in then, becoming clearly upset by the uproar. "What's going on?" he demanded.

"Mr. Goodman," Liza Ann said in a shaky voice, "I was putting my homework on your desk and when I returned to my desk, somebody had taken twenty-five dollars from my wallet."

"Don't you people realize what a common thing it is to have thefts around here?" Mr. Goodman snapped. "You're not little children. You ought to know never to leave a purse or a wallet unattended even for a moment. It's like leaving your sandwich out where the dog can get at it. I'm sorry, young lady, that you lost your money, but let it be a valuable lesson to you. Keep your valuables with you *at all times*."

"Yeah," Quincy Pierce chimed in, "my mom was shopping in the supermarket when we first moved here. She left her purse in the cart to go get some milk from the dairy section. Then when she got back, her purse was gone. She lost her credit cards, driver's license, money . . ."

"Exactly," Mr. Goodman affirmed. He looked around at the other students. "If any of you saw any suspicious activity around this girl's purse, by all means report what you saw to the office. Otherwise, there's nothing we can do. The police department has better things to do than track down thieving students."

"My handbag is on my shoulder every minute," Leticia said, directing a dirty look at Sereeta. "Nobody better try to rip me off."

Sereeta was a good math student, but today she didn't participate. She stared down at her textbook, lost in her own thoughts.

As they walked from the room after class, Quincy said to Sereeta, "That was really ugly for that girl to tell you to fork over the wallet—like you'd taken it. That made me mad."

"Thanks," Sereeta responded. "That's the second time this week I've been nearby when somebody was robbed."

"Yeah, me too," Quincy commented. "I guess we're unlucky. I'm super careful about the money I carry. My folks are really up against it. I couldn't afford to lose five dollars." Quincy looked sympathetically at Sereeta, "But I could afford to buy you an orange juice. They got really good orange juice in the machines. We have fifteen minutes before the next class. Want to get some juice?"

"Why not?" Sereeta agreed. She walked with Quincy to the beverage machine. He bought their juices and went outside, where it was hot in the sun. It was hot even under the trees, with the sun shining through the eucalyptus leaves. Quincy wore a T-shirt.

"Aren't you too warm in that sweatshirt, Sereeta?" Quincy asked.

"No," Sereeta replied, drinking the ice-cold orange juice. "Mmm, just hit the spot. Thanks, Quincy." Quincy smiled and nodded a "you're-welcome" to her, as he took off for his class. Sereeta's next class wouldn't start for almost ten minutes. So she walked on and found a quiet spot under the trees. She glanced around and then pulled off her sweatshirt, feeling cooler right away in the tank top she wore underneath. She ran her palm gently across the top of her arm. Then she took a deep breath, folded the sweat-shirt, and put it over her arm. After sitting a couple of minutes, she walked on to American History I.

Sereeta sat down next to Jaris in class. She laughed and said, "Isn't it awful what a bunch of thorny rosebushes will do to you when you try to prune them?"

Jaris looked at Sereeta's arm, at the healing cuts clearly made with a sharp, thin blade.

"What's the matter, Jaris?" Sereeta asked. "You're looking at me funny. Don't look at me like that. Everybody's treating me so strange. Don't you start too. My mother is treating me like a stranger, and my stepfather is treating me like an enemy. Some of the kids here at school are treating me like a thief. Don't you be looking at me funny too . . ."

"I'm sorry," Jaris apologized. "I was just thinking about something else. You know what, Sereeta? You should come over and have dinner at my house some night. That'd be fun. You could get away from your house while all that stuff is going on. My folks would love to have you over.

My pop, he's really something else. He got a cookbook that's got soul food recipes in it, and he's been going to town. He's making a special friend chicken, grits, sweet potato pie, everything down home. Mom doesn't cook much, you know. She's so busy with her teaching that she doesn't have time. We eat a lot of frozen dinners, you know. But with Pop hitting the kitchen, wow. He'll come home from the garage, wash up, put on that big hat and apron. He's in his glory. He's singing 'Ol' Man River,' and the pots and pans are banging. You oughta come over, Sereeta. He loves to show off to company."

Sereeta smiled. "That sounds awfully tempting. I'd love to be around some crazy, happy people for a change."

"How about tonight?" Jaris asked excitedly.

"I guess so," Sereeta agreed. "I don't exactly have a crowded social calendar. If I'm not home tonight, nobody will even miss me probably."

"Pop is picking me up from school this afternoon," Jaris told her. "He can pick you up too, and you can come home with us. I'll call him on my cell phone and tell him you're coming for dinner tonight."

"You can just do that?" Sereeta asked in amazement. "You can invite somebody to dinner at your house. And then just tell them company is coming and they should set another plate?"

"Sure," Jaris said, calling his father at Jackson's Auto Repair.

"Yeah," Pop answered. "If this is Mrs. Davis, your lemon of a Toyota isn't fixed yet, but I'm working on it. When you got a million miles on one of these old beaters, you gotta expect complicated repair jobs." Then Pop recognized Jaris's voice, and he said, "Oh, hey boy, how's it going? What's going down, boy?"

"Pop, Sereeta is coming for dinner tonight, okay?" Jaris asked. "She's really looking forward to it."

"Your friends are always welcome, boy, and when they're as pretty as Sereeta, va-va-voom. I'll tell Monie she needn't bother to put flowers on the table with Sereeta sitting there and prettying up the place."

Jaris and Pop ended their conversation. Jaris told Sereeta what his father had said. She smiled. "Can I have your father, Jaris? If you give him to me, I'll never ask you for anything else. I loved that beautiful gift of gold earrings you gave me for my birthday, but I'll even give them back if I can have your dad."

"Oh Pop has his faults," Jaris protested. "He gets these dark moods and he starts thinking his life is a big failure because he never went to college. He wanted to do something important in science. When he thinks he's probably going to be an auto mechanic for the rest of his life, he can get down. But all in all, Sereeta, I wouldn't trade him for anybody else's pop, that's for sure. He means the world to me."

"I hardly ever get to see my real father," Sereeta remarked. "Oh, he sends me birthday cards and Christmas gifts, and he says the usual fatherly things to me in his emails. But he's really happy with his new wife and his two stepsons. The boys are in Little League. They travel around to games, and it's like their life. Sometimes I forget what he looks like. I have to go look at his photograph, and even then he doesn't look familiar anymore."

"One of these days he'll probably come around to visit," Jaris assured her. But Jaris knew those were just words. A lot of men who remarry lose touch with their first families. Little by little they bond with the new family. And if the old family lives in a different town, the memories fade until the first children are practically strangers.

"I guess it's time for Ms. McDowell to come in and talk to us about President Bill Clinton," Sereeta noted, looking at the clock.

All the students were in the classroom now. They knew better than to be late for American history.

Jaris tried not to notice how some of the kids looked at Sereeta. Suspicion had been sown. Marko Lane walked in and said loud enough for everybody to hear, "Attention children, hang onto wallets, purses, and all other valuables. You hear what I'm saying? We are in dangerous territory."

Jasmine giggled, her gaze on Sereeta.

Ryann Kern said in a wounded voice, "I feel so terrible—a hundred dollars! My parents were so angry!"

Ms. McDowell came in then. All talking stopped. Discipline was a problem in some other classes, but not here. Never here.

CHAPTER THREE

When Jaris's father pulled up to Tubman High School that afternoon, Jaris and Sereeta were waiting. "Hop in, you guys," Pop told them. "I might not smell too good, but that's what comes of fixin' up old junkers all day. Every beater in town came through today, I figure. Old Jackson made enough to retire on just today."

"Thanks for inviting me to dinner," Sereeta said.

"Hey, I'm just getting into this cooking gig," Pop told her with a big grin. "I got me some high-class cookbooks. I'm watching some of these dudes on TV. I'm experimenting with everything. I never knew about stuff like thyme and oregano. But it makes the food taste great. You're never too old to learn. Who knows? Maybe when I get too old to monkey with cars I can be a chef. You know, like those guys on TV who make zillions for standing around marinating meat. You can sample some of my creations, tonight."

"No dinner out of the freezer tonight!" Jaris exclaimed.

"Yeah," Pop said. "My lady—Monie—she's a great girl, but she's a big shot teacher. She can't bother with cooking." He chuckled to himself.

"Jaris has told me what a good teacher his mom is," Sereeta commented.

"Oh yeah, she's good," Pop exclaimed. "The kids love her. But, like I tell her, what does an elementary teacher do? I call her a crayon jockey. She doesn't like that. But then she gets even with me. She calls me an engine ape." Pop laughed heartily, then he glanced at Sereeta. "I hear you got a new little brother in your house. That must be some trip."

"Yeah," Sereeta sighed, "it's different."

Pop gave Jaris a questioning look, and Jaris shrugged. Pop dropped the subject. Pop already knew that Sereeta was having problems adjusting to her new stepfather. He didn't yet know that the new family was beginning to crack and maybe come apart at the seams.

Later, at Jaris's house, Sereeta was in the living room talking to Chelsea when Jaris joined his parents in the kitchen. Mom was tossing the salad. Jaris briefly and quietly told them about the argument he overheard at the Manley house. "Sereeta is dealing with that," Jaris told them. "Now a couple kids at school had money stolen, and some freakin' fools have decided to blame Sereeta because she happened to be nearby when it happened—along with half a dozen other kids."

"High school can be a zoo," Pop remarked bitterly. "Tell me one other time in our lives when we're trapped in a place with a bunch of jerks who hate our guts.

And we can't get away from them. You got your bullies, and your snobs, your racists and your psychos, plus the regular kids just trying to survive. It's a dog-eat-dog world, man. Amazing that kids don't go directly from high school to the looney bin."

"Oh Lorenzo," Mom scolded. "It's not that bad. I spent some of the happiest times of my life in high school. I had lots of wonderful friends, and we had great fun times."

Pop rolled his eyes at Jaris. "Listen to Mary Poppins here," Pop complained. "She went to high school with the Cosby kids. Fat Albert was the cutup of the class. Aunt Jemima taught home ec. Everything was beautiful. She don't connect to the real world. She could land in a coven of witches, and she'd think they were sweet old ladies making fudge even as they load her into a cauldron of boiling water."

"Lorenzo!" Mom scolded in a sharper voice. "I am not naïve. I just refuse to focus on the dark side of everything like you do.

You're going to scar our kids' attitudes with that outlook."

Jaris's father began frying the chicken pieces and adding onions to the potatoes. He looked right at Jaris and said, "Level with me, boy. When you wake up in the morning, when you hear that old alarm go off and you remember it's a school day, does your stomach drop or what?"

Jaris didn't want to side with either parent, but at the moment he tended to agree with Pop, especially now with Sereeta under attack at school. He had fun times at Tubman High. But he also had a lot to worry about with tests, stress from people like Marko Lane, or just getting through another day and hoping nothing bad happened. "Maybe," Jaris thought, "Pop doesn't scar my mind with his dark thoughts. Maybe those dark thoughts are already in my DNA."

"Well," Jaris finally said out loud, "let's just say I'm not one of those guys who fly out of bed in the morning with a big grin on my face."

"Case closed," Pop declared, watching the chicken turn golden brown and crispy.

Later, as Pop put out what looked like a sumptuous feast, they all gathered around the table. "This sure beats the carton express, eh Monie?" Pop asked. Mom glared at Pop. He was at it again. He loved to call attention to her lack of cooking skills and frozen dinners. He liked to needle her. Jaris knew that after Sereeta went home, they would have another argument about how he loved to needle her. Pop would laugh things off and grab his wife and waltz her around the room and nibble on her ear. All the while, she would laugh while trying not to.

"Some of the TV dinners are pretty good," Jaris announced out of loyalty to his mother. "The shrimp casserole is okay."

"Except for those little green pebbles they call peas," Chelsea interjected.

Sereeta giggled. Jaris was glad to see that. He had not seen her giggle in a long time. He was glad she could forget all the bad things going on in her life for a little while and just giggle.

When they had finished dinner and were having dessert—sweet potato pie—Pop turned to Sereeta and said, "Jaris tells me some kids been rippin' each other off at your school. That's another thing you got to expect in high school. Lot of thieving going on. You lay something down, you kiss it good-bye."

"It's just that it's happened twice in two days," Sereeta replied. "This girl, Ryann Kern, she's really smart and sort of a loner. Her parents gave her a hundred dollars to shop for summer clothes and it was stolen. She left her purse leaning on the base of Harriet Tubman's statue, she said, and then looked away and it happened. Ryann was crying and everything. I felt so bad. And then some kids started looking at me as if I was the one who took the money—and I could have died."

"Those little weasels," Pop remarked. "They love to rat kids out. I remember being in this science class back in the Stone Age when I went to high school, and we were looking at slides with these microscopes. This teacher, he really loved his scopes. He said if any of us jerks damaged one of his scopes, we better run for our lives. You know, bumping the lens into the slides, stuff like that. Well, we got this poor doofus in the class and sure enough he cracks one of the lenses. He's looking at this amoeba, and he twists it down too far and *kar-unch*, it breaks. Man, this kid is like having a stroke. Well, he darts away from the microscope, and he's hoping nobody knows who busted it. But when the teacher comes in, there's half a dozen jerks ratting him out. They all go, 'Hey, teach, Hank busted your microscope.'"

"Yeah," Sereeta agreed, "this one girl, Jasmine. She came right out and said I stole the money."

"She's the little witch who hangs out with that weirdo Marko Lane, right?" Pop asked. "Jaris tells me about what a bully he is. Well, birds of a feather . . ."

Mom had been quietly eating, but now she joined the conversation. "Sereeta, you have to ignore people like that Jasmine. You know you didn't do anything wrong, and if people like her are saying cruel and nasty things about you, just ignore them. That's their problem," Mom asserted.

Chelsea shook her head violently. "No, Mom, it's Sereeta's problem. Last year a girl in my class brought in this old book from her grandfather, and she said it was like an heirloom or something. It got stolen and everybody blamed poor Bernice Jones, and it got so bad Bernice's parents had to pull her out of school."

"Well, it won't come to that with Sereeta," Mom declared, turning to Sereeta. "You have so many wonderful friends at school, sweetie. You don't have to worry about a few bad apples gossiping about you."

Pop looked at Jaris and suggested, "Be good if you could figure out who's doing the stealing. You say a couple of kids have lost money, pretty quick, one after another? That means some kid is anxious for money—real anxious—willing to dip into other kids' stuff, you hear what I'm saying? Maybe somebody is feeding a drug problem or something."

Jaris had already gone over all the students who were in the area of the thefts. He had thought about each one and ruled most of them out at once. Alonee and Sami he trusted completely. He wasn't sure about Quincy, and he had his suspicions about Jasmine. Jaris tended to think Jasmine didn't need money, though. That left Quincy, but he seemed like such a nice guy.

After dinner, Pop drove Sereeta home, and Jaris came along. But when they got to the Manley house, no lights were on.

"That's funny," Sereeta commented. "Everybody is supposed to be home. They were planning to watch a TV show they liked tonight."

Jaris, Pop, and Sereeta walked up the flagstone path to the large porch that fronted the house. Although it had been remodeled, the house had been built many years earlier when large front porches were common.

When they reached the porch, they heard the soft whimper of a baby. It came from the darkness of the porch. They also heard the faint whine of the swing going back and forth. When Sereeta was a little girl, she and her friends loved to sit in the swing, especially on warm nights.

Jaris made out the form of someone sitting in the swing. As he got closer, he recognized Olivia Manley with her baby in her lap. "Hello, Mrs. Manley," Jaris said nervously. "We brought Sereeta home . . . she had dinner at my house . . . and now we're . . . home."

Jaris's father went up on the porch. He asked Mrs. Manley if she was all right.

"I'm fine," the woman replied. "Thank you for having my daughter to dinner. That was very nice."

"Where's Perry, Mom?" Sereeta asked. Her stepfather's car was not in the driveway, where he usually parked.

"Oh, my husband is on a business trip," Mrs. Manley answered in a strange, light voice.

"When is he coming back?" Sereeta asked.

"I'm not sure," she said. She turned her attention to Jaris's father. "You're Olivia's husband, aren't you? My, you're very handsome. I haven't seen you in a long time. How are you?"

"Okay," Pop answered. He looked at Jaris with a funny expression on his face. He raised his eyebrows. There was a bottle of alcohol—partly full—on the floor near Olivia Manley's feet.

"My goodness, what a handsome man you are," Mrs. Manley said again. "Olivia knew how to pick them. Remember when we were all first married? I was married to Tom then. Oh, how young and foolish we all were. How time flies . . . and now . . . and now . . . One day we are young like those two, like your son and my daughter . . . " Mrs. Manley waved her hand in the air like a bird.

49

Jaris looked at Sereeta. Sereeta announced tersely, "She's drunk."

"And the next thing you know, you're
not young anymore," Mrs. Manley went on,
not hearing Sereeta. "You look in the mirror,
and there's a stranger there with lines in her
face and horrid little crow's feet around
her eyes and you ask, 'Who are you?' "

"Mom, I'll put the baby to bed, okay?"
Sereeta suggested.

"Would you, dear? I'm rather tired." Mrs.
Manley turned to Pop: "Oh, Lorenzo, say
hello to Livy. Tell her we need to go shopping
together again. It's been much too long."

Sereeta took the baby and went in the
house. Jaris followed her. When they were
alone in the baby's room, he asked softly,
"Is there anything I can do?"

"I'll just put him in his crib," Sereeta
said. "It looks like he's had his bottle. I'll
put him on his back and he'll sleep. You're
supposed to put them on their backs."

"Are you going to be okay here,
Sereeta?" Jaris asked her.

"Yes," Sereeta said, putting the baby down and tucking him in. "My mother'll be all right in the morning. And Perry will be home. He didn't go on a business trip. They must have had another fight and he just left for a while." As she spoke, Jaris noticed all the mobiles hanging from the ceiling. He had never seen such a beautiful baby's room. The little toy baseballs and basketballs were everywhere. The balloons clung to the ceiling, shrunken now. They still said, "Welcome Home, Jake."

Then Sereeta turned toward Jaris with a terrible expression on her face. "You don't know how much I hated him—the baby. I blamed him for taking all my mother's attention away from me. I thought she didn't even care enough for me to come see me in that play I was so proud of. And it was all the baby's fault. They made this wonderland for him. All the decorations, the mobiles, the toys. It was like the little prince was coming, their true child. And I was the hated stepdaughter that nobody cared about. But I was all wrong, Jaris. They don't . . . they don't . . . really care for him either." Her voice broke and tears ran down her face.

Jaris walked over and took Sereeta in his arms. He held her tightly and kissed her. "Hang in there, babe. Just hang in there. It'll be okay," he consoled her.

When Jaris got back downstairs, Sereeta's mother was talking to Pop. "I still remember the senior prom, when I was Sereeta's age." She sounded drowsy. "I was so beautiful . . . so beautiful . . . it isn't fair, is it?"

"You know what?" Pop said to her. "You got to pull yourself together for your kids, lady. You hear what I'm sayin' to you, Olivia? You got a sixteen-year-old girl who needs a mother bad. She's in a world of hurt, and she needs a mother. And that baby, he needs a mom too. You gotta step up to the plate, girlie. You gotta start forgettin' about the prom you went to a hundred years ago, and start being a mother to your kids."

Olivia Manley stared at the man before her. "Why, you are very rude!" she cried.

"Yeah, well listen," Pop growled. "Somebody's got to take care of business around here. I don't know if that jerk Perry is coming back or not, but it doesn't do for you to be sittin' out here in the dark with a baby and drinking yourself into a stupor."

"You are really mean," the woman whispered hoarsely. "Poor Monica with a cruel husband like you. I thought you were a gentleman but you're not. You're a cruel, harsh man to accuse me of drinking when liquor has not touched my lips for ages."

Pop went up the porch steps. He snatched up the bottle and poured the remaining liquor onto the lawn. Then he put the empty bottle in the blue recycling bin.

"Oh, you dreadful man!" Olivia Manley sobbed.

"Go in the house and go to bed, Olivia," Jaris's father said. He turned to Jaris. "Is Sereeta gonna be okay with the baby?"

"Yeah, she says so," Jaris said. "She has my cell number if she needs me, if something comes up."

Olivia Manley got to her feet and walked slowly to the door. She stood a moment looking at Jaris and his father. "I . . . I d-don't deserve this," she sobbed before going inside and slamming the door.

Jaris and his father walked back to the pickup. They didn't talk on the way home.

Jaris was scared, and he tried to sort out his feelings. Sereeta was so fragile. The situation in her home was much worse than he had imagined. And she was going to that vacant lot where the house had burned down, sitting on those blackened foundation stones, and cutting herself. She was talking about a family long ago who died in a fire, and she was thinking it had been a good thing. She was feeling their spirits in the ruins and thinking a tragedy had been somehow good.

"Pop," Jaris asked when they were almost home, "what are we supposed to do?"

Pop was tightly gripping the wheel. "I don't know," he said. "It might be okay. Maybe the jerk'll come back, and they'll make up and work it out. Maybe he has more sense than she does". Then he added, "It's been hard on that girl. Real hard. You can see it in her eyes. You know what I'm saying, boy? She looks like she's quitting . . . I can see how she's holding on with all her might, but a part of her wants to quit . . ." He shook his head. Jaris stared straight ahead into the darkness. He could still feel Sereeta in his arms, soft and tender and fragile, a broken doll.

CHAPTER FOUR

In the morning on Wednesday, as Jaris walked toward Harriet Tubman's statue, he saw Ryann Kern and Leticia Hicks walking together. They were always together. They were the tightest pair in the junior class. Other juniors had close friends, but sometimes you'd see them with other people. Not Ryann and Leticia. They tried to sit together in classes they shared. They ate lunch together. Both were born in a small town in Alabama. They moved with their families to the Tubman neighborhood about three years ago. Jaris figured they never quite felt at home here, so they stuck together.

Jaris heard the pair whispering behind him. When he turned and looked back, they had strange looks on their faces. He guessed they were saying something like, "There's that Sereeta's boyfriend. He probably knows she took the money, and he's covering for her. These crooked city kids stick together."

Jaris turned and asked, "You never found the money you lost, huh Ryann?"

"I didn't lose it," Ryann snapped. "It was stolen."

"I think it's a shame people can get away with something like that," Leticia added.

Just then Tarina Peters, a cheerleader at Tubman High, came running up. "Did you hear? The carwash money is gone!" she screamed. All the students streaming into Tubman for morning classes gathered around Tarina to hear the sad story. On Saturday, to raise money for summer cheerleader camp, the cheerleaders ran a car wash in the supermarket parking lot. Girls stood on surrounding street corners, waving signs announcing the car wash. The money was collected in a steel box, and two mothers were in charge of it. When the cash was officially counted Sunday night, the total was about two hundred dollars short of what was supposed to be in the box.

"And they're trying to keep things quiet," Tarina finished her story, "'cause they have to talk with everybody that was there. But I just heard about it from somebody on the team."

"Who was watchin' the till," Sami Archer asked.

"Suzy Pierce, Quincy's mom, and Jasmine's mom, Lee," Tarina answered.

Jasmine came charging over. "It wasn't my mom's fault," she insisted. "It was so mixed up and disorganized that people were throwin' in money and trying to make their own change. But my mom kept a tight rein anyway. When she turned that box over to Quincy's mom, all the money was accounted for."

"If *my* mom had been in charge, no money would be missin'," Sami chimed in. "She'd of made sure everything was done right."

"You don't know what you're talkin' about, girl," Jasmine yelled. "Don't go talkin' trash about my mom. Your mom is a big fat lazy—"

That was all she got to say before Sami's hand smacked her face. Jasmine flew backward, almost falling into a hedge. Jaris was close enough to grab her, breaking her fall. He held on to her as she struggled to get at Sami. Trevor Jenkins grabbed Sami, who was rushing at Jasmine for a second round.

"You guys wanna get busted for fighting?" Jaris yelled. "If the teachers see you chicks going at each other, you're both toast!"

Jasmine touched her red and smarting face, and she snarled a warning to Sami. "Sami Archer, if you ever hit me again, I swear I'll break your fat neck. You just stay away from me if you don't want big trouble."

"You ain't getting by with insulting my mom," Sami yelled back. "You can insult me all you want, but my mom is off limits, girl. *Nobody* insults my mom without getting bruised!"

"Cool it, girls!" Jaris insisted. "You're lucky no teacher was around."

Jasmine glared at Jaris, "You know what, Jaris? Your girlfriend, Sereeta, she was helping wave those signs for the car wash. I saw her near the cash box when Quincy's mother was working it," she said. "She coulda helped herself to the cash box real easy."

"You're reaching, Jasmine," Jaris responded. "You're mad at me because Sami is my friend."

"My mother did a good job on her turn with the cash box," Jasmine asserted. "My mother worked hard. Quincy's mom's not the sharpest knife in the drawer, if you get my meaning. Anything coulda got by her."

The other students disappeared, disappointed that the catfight didn't go on longer. Derrick Shaw shook his head and smiled, "Man, when girls go at it, it's something else. You see guys fightin' and it's nothin' compared to a coupla chicks going head to head."

Just before the last bell, the principal of Tubman High issued a statement over the PA system:

> We are very sorry to tell our students and their parents that there has been a rash of thefts from purses at our school. Apparently someone has also stolen partial proceeds from the cheerleader's benefit car wash held on Saturday. We cannot overemphasize the need to keep a close watch on all valuables. If you have any information concerning these unfortunate events, please come to the office. Your identity will be kept confidential.

Leaving the school building, Jaris noticed Quincy Pierce standing on the edge of the campus. He looked very upset. As Jaris went by and nodded to him, Quincy said, "I suppose you think it's my mom's fault too. Everybody's blaming my mom that the cheerleader money is gone."

"No," Jaris protested, "I don't think anything. I don't know enough about it."

"They don't like us around here," Quincy went on, "my folks and me. I was nearby when both girls got their purses rifled, and my mom was watching the money at the car wash. Kids are thinking me and my mom are thieves or something. We're new around here, and we don't live in a nice house. People look down on us. It's easy to think we're poor, so we're probably thieves too. My folks are really struggling. Dad's been sick, and we got a lot of doctor and hospital bills we can't pay. We got bill collectors hounding us all the time. Yeah, we got problems, but that doesn't mean we're crooks."

Jaris tried to make him feel better. "Probably whoever is doing the stealing doesn't even need the money. They're probably doing it for kicks. Lotta shoplifters are like that. They take stuff because they can."

An old car rattled up to them.

"That's my mom," Quincy explained. "She's picking me up today 'cause Dad's in the hospital and we're visiting him."

Jaris walked over to the car window. "Hello Mrs. Pierce," Jaris said, "I hope your husband is better soon."

"Thanks," the weary looking woman at the wheel sighed, "but nothin' goin' good for us. Lordy, my man's sick, and bills all over like cockroaches. I volunteered to help with that school car wash, and look what's come 'a that. It's like a curse is on us or sump'n. It's enough to make you wanna pack it in and lay down by the river and die. I'm no good at keepin' money straight. Tens and fives all look alike. Pretty little teenager come over to try to sort things out, putting the money in different compartments, but it was too late."

"Your girlfriend, Sereeta Prince," Quincy explained. "That's who she's talking about. She came over to help Mom. She's a nice girl. I bought her an orange juice on that hot day. Course, you never can tell. Maybe she's not as nice as she looks . . . maybe she wasn't really helping Mom."

Quincy drove off with his mother, leaving Jaris standing at the curb with a sick feeling in the pit of his stomach. It wasn't a good thing that Sereeta tried to sort the money. What if some of the kids who mistrusted her anyway saw her and started spreading more gossip?

Jaris walked across the campus, wondering if Sereeta was already on her way home. She often walked, as Jaris did. He hoped she had not taken the long way, behind the pizza place, to that vacant field with the ruins of the burned house.

Jaris started home, at first jogging and hoping to catch up to Sereeta. He was in luck. He saw her just ahead, walking along. "Hey Sereeta!" he shouted. "Wait up."

Sereeta stopped and waited for him. She told him earlier, in American history, that things at her house had settled down. Mom had a bad hangover, but Perry was home. Things were relatively quiet. But Jaris had not talked to Sereeta yet about the missing car wash money.

"Yeah, how awful," she remarked about the missing car wash money. "I tried to help Mrs. Pierce when I saw bills flying all over the blacktop. I tried to explain to her how to put the different denominations in the compartments. I thought I was doing a good thing. Now I'm not so sure. I mean, there's enough gossip about me already."

"Probably the money just blew away," Jaris suggested.

"Jaris, remember that story 'The String' that we read in Mr. Pippin's class at the beginning of the year?" Sereeta asked.

"Yeah, I remember," Jaris responded. "The harness maker guy stopped to pick up a piece of string and just at that time some guy lost his pocketbook."

"Right," Sereeta went on, "and people were looking and when the harness maker stooped, they just figured he was picking up the pocketbook to steal it. Well, he wasn't, but everybody started seeing him as a thief.

And then in the story, remember? The guy found his pocketbook and everybody knew the harness maker hadn't taken it, but yet they continued to call him a thief. He had just lost his reputation and he couldn't get it back."

"I see where you're going with this, Sereeta," Jaris commented, "but that was just a story."

"Yeah, but what is Mr. Pippin always saying? Art imitates life. I just feel like everybody wants to believe I'm involved in this stupid stuff at school," Sereeta protested.

"No, they don't," Jaris insisted. "A few kids—"

"Do you remember how the harness maker's story ended?" Sereeta interrupted. "He couldn't face what had happened so he went to bed and died."

"Come on, Sereeta!" Jaris demanded. "They're going to get to the bottom of this thieving stuff, and then we'll all know what happened."

They continued walking. Across the street was the vacant lot with the burned houses. Sereeta glanced in that direction and said, "I found an old history book with local lore in it. It told all about this neighborhood, how the streets are named for Indian tribes . . . and then it tells about that burned house."

"Yeah?" Jaris said, not sure he wanted to hear the story.

"A young couple built the house. It was one of the first houses around here. They'd been married just a few months when the girl got sick. She knew she was very sick, but she didn't have the heart to tell her husband because they were so much in love. She knew it'd hurt him terribly. They were really young, like teenagers . . . And she agonized over how she'd tell him. So she decided she'd cook a dinner for him, a nice dinner, and afterward she'd tell him she was going to die. She put all this in her diary and she kept the diary in the concrete floor, in a secret block. But then something happened

with the stove while she was cooking dinner, and the house burned down. They both
died that night. The house was gone, but the
foundation stones survived, and they found
the diary years later. They put the story in
this book."

"That's a sad story," Jaris commented.

"No, it's not really," Sereeta objected.
"She never had to tell him she was dying.
He never had to be hurt in that way. That's
why sometimes when I feel their spirits, I
sense a peace and happiness."

Jaris stopped walking. He turned to
Sereeta and took her hands in his. "Babe, I
worry about you sometimes. Do you know
that? I spend a lot of time worrying about
you because sometimes you seem very sad
and gloomy."

"Oh, don't worry about me," Sereeta
protested. "I'm all right."

"I don't think so," Jaris insisted. "I care
about you a lot, but you won't really talk to
me. I know the way it is with your family
has hurt you a lot, and I can't do anything

about that. But you know, if you feel really desperate, you need to come to me and not ever do stupid things. We can be together and forget about the stupid stuff, you know? Sometimes when my Pop gets really down about his place in life, how his dreams all got busted, it gets me down too. And what's helped me get out of the dark place I fall into is being with you, Sereeta. You lift me up. I want to do that for you, babe. You hear what I'm telling you?"

"I'm glad I've made you happier," Sereeta said.

"I want to make you happier too, babe," Jaris insisted.

"You do," she replied.

"But not enough," Jaris said. He wanted to ask why she got so desperate that she cut herself and didn't come to him. But he couldn't bring that up. "You gotta lean on me, babe. When you're down, don't go sit in some empty field and look at burned stones and think about sad stuff that happened a hundred years ago. Think of you and me."

"I will," Sereeta promised.

They walked on, beyond the field, to the corner of Sereeta's street. They walked down the street, and near her house they stopped. The house was lit up.

"See, it's all okay tonight," Jaris declared. He drew Sereeta close to him and kissed her. She kissed him back, lingering in the moment.

"Remember what I told you in that hospital room when you gave me the earrings, Jaris?" she asked.

"Yeah, you said you loved me," he said.

"I do," she said softly, before turning up the flagstone walk to her door.

In the twilighted neighborhood, Jaris continued on to his house, about a mile from Sereeta's. He jogged part of the way. He felt a little better. Sereeta seemed calmer, more at peace.

As he ran, he figured surely everybody at school would be extra careful about leaving purses and wallets lying around. Whoever the thief was would get discouraged and maybe stop stealing. Then the thing would blow over. The thief had to know that you can't keep on ripping people off at the same location and avoid being caught.

When Jaris got home, Mom was working on the computer and Pop was working late at the garage. "Honey!" Mom called out to Jaris when she heard the door close. "Just get something in the freezer for you and Chelsea, will you? I'm really hammered on this work. I got some new stuff—fish sticks and mashed potatoes. They looked really good. You could cup up a melon too. Thanks!"

Jaris and Chelsea looked in the refrigerator together. Jaris assessed the dinner situation: "Okay, cardboard chicken or plywood turkey or those new fish sticks. I bet they taste just like the chicken and the turkey. It's your call, chili pepper."

Chelsea giggled. "Look, some old pizza is left over. Couldn't we warm it up? Even if it burns, it's better than that other stuff."

"You got it, girl," Jaris said. "Warmed over pizza it is. Old pizza pie rules." He chopped up the melon to eat with the pizza. It turned out to be a pretty nice meal, especially when Jaris added vanilla ice cream to the cut-up fruit.

As they sat eating, Chelsea chattered to Jaris. "You know that girl in your school who lost the hundred dollars? Ryann Kern? Well, her sister goes to my school. Her name is Gloria. She told me that her mom and dad felt so bad about Ryann losing the hundred dollars that they gave her another hundred. Her dad had to borrow it from the credit union so Ryann could go get her summer clothes. Gloria was really freaked out about that. She said if Ryann is too stupid to hang on to a hundred dollars, then she should go without new summer clothes and wear last summer's clothes."

"I'm with Gloria," Jaris agreed, between munches.

"You know what else?" Chelsea went on. "That Liza Ann who lost the twenty-five when somebody reached in her purse? She's Ryann's and Gloria's cousin. She went crying to her parents sayin' her cousin got the money back from her parents. She wanted her twenty-five back. But her mom told her to go jump in the creek—that next time maybe she'll watch her money better." Chelsea laughed.

"Good for Liza Ann's parents," Jaris said.

"I wonder who stole the cheerleader's money, Jare," Chelsea mused. "Do you think the same crook who got money from those girls' purses took the car wash money?"

"I don't know," Jaris replied. "It's sure got a lot of kids upset. Everybody's looking over their shoulders all the time and hanging on extra tight to their stuff."

"Somebody at my school said Sereeta took the stuff," Chelsea remarked. "But I told her she was a dirty liar."

CHAPTER FIVE

On Friday, Jaris heard angry voices coming from the lunch area near the eucalyptus trees. Two guys seemed to be hotly arguing under the trees. As Jaris drew closer, he made out Marko Lane's angry voice and Quincy Pierce's defensive tone. It sounded like Marko was getting the best of the argument.

"Listen up, dude," Marko was demanding. "My chick don't like her mom gettin' in hot water over this. Jasmine is real ticked that her mom is takin' the heat over that missing car wash money. Your old lady was on duty when the money disappeared, man. Jasmine's mom is a smart lady with an office job. She knows how to keep money straight. Either your mom took the money to pay all those bills you guys got, or else—"

"My mom is no thief," Quincy said heatedly. "She doesn't handle money. She's a cleaning lady. She's not used to having money coming at her that fast—"

"Okay," Marko interrupted, "then why did she offer to work at the car wash in the first place? If she's so stupid she can't count money, she got no business doin' the job, dude."

"She's not stupid!" Quincy groaned. "She's just not good at some things. Anyway—what about Sereeta who came to help her? Maybe she took the money."

Jaris froze. Quincy was ready to throw Sereeta to the wolves to get his mother off the hook. Quincy's voice went on eagerly. "Sereeta Prince, she was handling all the money and telling Mom what to do. But maybe she saw all that money and just . . . took . . . some . . ."

Jaris stepped up and announced, "You guys, Sereeta was trying to be helpful.

She wouldn't take a nickel of anybody's money."

"That's what you say, dude," Marko sneered, "'cause she's your chick now. But two hundred dollars is missing from that money box. So Jasmine's mom got a call from the cheerleader coach that she needs to come in and explain what all was going on. Jasmine's mom has a lot of pride, and she don't like this one bit. I'm wanting to help my chick. You get my meaning?"

"You can't blame it on Sereeta," Jaris insisted. "Maybe people were giving out the wrong change. Maybe somebody handed in a ten, and somebody gave them back a twenty."

"My mother wouldn't have made that many mistakes," Quincy argued. "Not two hundred dollars worth." Quincy looked miserable. He was a nice guy. He didn't want to get Sereeta in trouble. He liked her. But he was afraid the school people would come after his mother and make her come up with the missing two hundred dollars.

CHAPTER FIVE

The Pierce family didn't have that kind of money. They couldn't spare twenty dollars. Quincy thought it just wasn't fair. His mother, with all her troubles, had volunteered her time to help out with a school project. Now they were going to interview her along with Jasmine's mother.

"Sereeta said she saw bills flying all over the parking lot when she walked up," Jaris said.

"My mom wouldn't have let that happen!" Quincy seemed near tears.

"Well," Marko snarled, "I'm tellin' you one thing. Some stupid lady who can't count to ten, and a thievin' chick ain't gonna be the duo that brings down Jasmine's mom. When Jasmine's mom goes in to talk to those people, she's gonna be up front. She's gonna say this Mrs. Pierce is too dumb to come in outta the rain, and they had no business letting her handle the money. And then along comes this Sereeta chick to get her hands in the bills up to her elbows, and it was bad all around."

Jaris felt sick. Marko was out to protect Jasmine's mother, and Quincy was protecting his mom. The both of them had to somehow put the blame on Sereeta, to make it look like she'd helped herself to two hundred dollars that belonged to the Tubman cheerleaders.

At that moment, Jaris remembered that story "The String." Sereeta's fear seemed to be coming true after all. Innocence was no protection for the harness maker in the story, and it seemed no protection for Sereeta either.

That same morning, Quincy's mother had to take time off from work to talk to the physical education department chairman, who was handling the investigation. The school officials had not yet contacted the police because they were not sure if there had been an error in counting the money or a theft. Mrs. Pierce admitted that she was confused while she handled the money, but she swore that she could not have made two hundred dollars worth of mistakes.

Then Jasmine's mother, sharp looking in black slacks and a red sweater, appeared. She marched into the office like a soldier going on duty. Jaris learned later that she had laid the blame on Mrs. Pierce and Sereeta, not herself.

At midday, Sereeta was asked to talk to the PE chairman. "I have to see him at two o'clock," Sereeta told Jaris. "I'm really nervous."

After school, Jaris saw Sereeta. She looked as if she had been crying, although her eyes were now dry. They went across the street to the local teen hangout and sat in the corner drinking diet colas.

"They talked to me for about twenty minutes," Sereeta told Jaris. "They were nice and everything. They just asked me how the money was being kept and stuff like that. I don't know if they were thinking I took it. . . . I felt so horrible. I mean, nobody has ever suspected me of anything dishonest before . . . it feels so awful."

"There've been a lot of rumors," Jaris admitted. "But it'll be over pretty soon. They'll find out what really happened, and then you'll be fine."

"Yeah, like the harness maker in 'The String' was fine," Sereeta moaned.

"Sereeta," Jaris said, "my sister Chelsea, she goes to school with Ryann's sister, and you know those parents replaced that hundred for Ryann? They had to borrow the money from the credit union, but they replaced it. Then the other girl, Liza Ann, she wanted her money replaced, but her parents refused."

"Wouldn't it be funny if the girls didn't lose the money in the first place and just played a trick to get more money from their parents?" Sereeta suggested. "I mean, of course that didn't happen, but it'd be some con, wouldn't it?" A look of bitterness crossed Sereeta's face. "You know, the rumors about me having something to do with the missing money got to my stepfather at his office. Somebody he works with has a daughter in the freshman class at Tubman. Anyway, he was really angry. He asked me if there was any truth to the accusations. He actually looked at me and asked me if I had done anything dishonest. He acted like he was the judge and I was the accused. He raved on and on about his wonderful reputation and how important that is for an executive who handles money. I've never liked him, but I hated him when he asked me all those questions. It was so humiliating. I cussed him out, Jaris. Then I went to my room and cried."

Jaris reached across the table and covered Sereeta's hand with his. "Lean on me, babe," he urged her.

"I'm in their way," Sereeta confided. "More than Jake. They can dump Jake in a day care for infants. He'll be like a teddy bear in storage. They have him, but they don't. They can look him up again when he's seven or something. But I'm a messy teenager. I'm causing trouble. Now I'm even embarrassing Perry Manley by stealing money from the cheerleaders."

"What did your mom say when he accused you?" Jaris asked.

"She tried to defend me—feebly. Then she got drunk," Sereeta replied. "You know, I remember when everything was so good at my house. It seemed good to me anyway. My real father lived there, and we went on picnics and stuff. Mom didn't drink much, just wine at meals. Every day was just really good. I liked school and I was doing okay. I had nice friends. I wonder some-times why everyday I didn't say, 'Wow, I'm so happy.' But I was too dumb to know how happy I was, how good it was."

"It'll be good again for you, Sereeta," Jaris assured her.

"No, it won't be like it was. Not ever. I'll never have a family again. Not a kid's family, I mean. I hope I get a family of my own that'll be good. I'll be a nice mom, and I'll love my kids to pieces, and my husband will love me and the kids. We'll post their drawings on the fridge with magnets . . . And we'll make a big deal of everything they do." Tears began to run down her face.

"Come home with me again tonight, Sereeta," Jaris pleaded.

"No, I'm okay. I'm fine," she said.

Out of the corner of his eye, Jaris saw Quincy enter. In that same moment, Quincy spotted Jaris and Sereeta. A look of pure guilt and misery came over Quincy's face. He walked, haltingly, over to where Sereeta and Jaris sat.

"Sereeta," Quincy began, "my mom talked to the school people, but she didn't say anything bad about you. Mom just said she was not good with money, and maybe she made some mistakes. But she couldn't have made so many that two hundred dollars is gone . . . "

Sereeta looked at Quincy but said nothing.

"Sereeta," he continued, "I'm sorry about everything. Nobody thinks you took the money, except maybe for some jerks.

I'm sorry if I said anything that hurt you. I was just . . . just so scared for my mom."

Sereeta said nothing, and Quincy eventually walked away.

"I may hang out with my grandmother," Sereeta told Jaris. "That always helps."

"Yeah, that's a good idea," Jaris agreed. "She's your real dad's mom I know, but I wonder if he ever tells her he's coming around to see you and her . . ."

"No, she hasn't seen him in a long time either," Sereeta explained. "He's changed, Jaris. His new wife is very domineering and sets the rules. Life is all about her two boys now." Then Sereeta glanced at the clock on the wall. "Oh, I'm riding home with Alonee tonight, remember? We're both getting haircuts at that new place. We want it shorter for summer. Then Alonee's dad will drop me home. So . . . see you in the morning, Jaris."

Jaris watched Sereeta walk out.

Jaris racked his brain for a way to figure out what happened with the thefts at school. He had to find a way to clear Sereeta completely.

Jaris's suspicions kept returning to Jasmine. She was nearby every time money disappeared. It would have been so easy for her to walk up to her mother at the car wash cash counter, distract her, and take the two hundred. Jasmine's family was prosperous, but her father was pretty strict with money. Jasmine didn't get everything she wanted.

When Jaris got home from school, his mother approached him. "Honey, Ms. McDowell just called. You didn't turn in some important project that was due today. She was really surprised. You've *never* missed a deadline before."

Jaris clapped his hand to his forehead. "Oh man! That thing on Clinton. I totally forgot about that. I did most of the research on the Internet, and I read two books on it. I was almost done and then I let it go!" Jaris was between an A and a B in American history. If he did well on this project, he thought he had a good shot at an A.

"Ms. McDowell said if you turn it in before class tomorrow morning, you can still get credit, Jaris," Mom told him.

"Okay Mom, thanks, I'll get right at it," Jaris assured her.

"Jaris," Mom commented, worry lining her brow. "You have not been yourself the last few weeks. I talk to you, and your mind is a million miles away. Is everything all right?"

"You know, Mom," Jaris answered, "this stealing at school and some jerks blaming Sereeta. It's really gotten to me. She feels terrible and I feel terrible for her."

"Sweetie," Mom said, "I know you care deeply for Sereeta, but you can't let her problems drive you over a cliff, okay?"

"If I could only find out who's doing the stealing," Jaris said.

"You aren't the police, and you're not a private investigator, Jaris," Mom told him. "Sereeta has got to pull herself together. I feel sorry for her too. I wish Olivia could be more of a mother to her. But I'm concerned about you, sweetie. You're my baby. I want you to do well in school and have a bright future. I don't want you to be like your father, spending years regretting the things he never got to do. You've got to keep focused on your own future."

Pop came into view then. He was getting dinner ready, and he had gravy all over his apron. "What's wrong, Jaris?" he asked.

"Same old, Pop," Jaris replied. "They haven't solved those thefts at school, and they're casting suspicion on Sereeta. The PE people questioned her today."

"She's getting a raw deal, that kid is," Pop declared with a strong vein of righteous anger in his voice. "They got no right to be running a deal on her like that. They got no evidence. They're way off base questioning her—a sixteen-year-old kid—like some criminal. What've they got? Some punks saying she was near the little idiots who lost their money? What's that mean? If I'm walking alongside a building that's on fire, does that mean I started the freakin' fire?"

Jaris appreciated his father getting angry. Jaris was angry too, and it made him feel better to see Pop riled up. That was one of the things that Jaris loved about his father—his sense of justice. Even if somebody else suffered an injustice, Pop was as angry as if he were the victim.

"Boy," Pop went on, "you tell that little girl she doesn't have to answer their stupid questions anymore. She didn't do anything wrong. Those fools shoulda watched their purses better. The ladies who ran the money box during the car wash were idiots. How is any of that the fault of a sixteen-year-old kid who's already got her plate full of trouble? Next time they want to talk to her, you tell her to tell them to take a long walk off a short pier. You tell that little girl they're just blowin' smoke. They screwed up over there, putting a couple of crazy ladies in charge of a money box, and now they want to take it out of a kid's hide."

Pop fumed his way back into the kitchen.

Jaris looked at his mother. "Pop is awesome," he remarked.

Mom smiled. "Well, there had to be some reason I married him beside the fact that he was the handsomest boy who asked me out."

After dinner that evening, Jaris hurried to his room then and got started on finishing his project on President Clinton. He sat at the computer for two hours and then printed it out. It was a good report. He had worked on it for two weeks, and he thought it deserved an A—if he hadn't been late with it.

When Jaris went to bed, he couldn't sleep. He was too tense. He'd put so much into winding up the report that he couldn't slow down enough to sleep. And then there was Sereeta. He desperately wanted to do something to make it all better for her. But he sickeningly knew that he lacked the power to make any of it better.

CHAPTER SIX

The theft problem struck again on Wednesday of the following week, in American history. Ms. McDowell had not yet begun the class. She was just putting her briefcase down.

Bekka Crandall let out a shriek and began pawing furiously in her purse. "It's missing!" she cried. "The fifty dollars Mom gave me this morning for shopping is missing!"

Ms. McDowell looked down at the junior who sat in the second row. She asked her calmly, "You've lost some money, Bekka?"

"No ma'am," Bekka protested. "Somebody had to have stolen it, ma'am. It was right here in my purse. I showed it to my friends, Jenna and Luci right here. Mom gave it to me this morning. It was a birthday gift from my grandmother in South Carolina."

"We saw the money," the other girls said.

"I showed it to them, then I put it back in my wallet, Ms. McDowell," Bekka explained. "Now there's just a couple old dollars bouncing around in my wallet. I keep my purse under my desk, and most likely somebody reached in there and took it, ma'am."

"Bekka," the teacher asked, still calmly, "are you sure you didn't put the fifty dollar bill in another compartment of your purse when you put it back?"

"No ma'am. I'm sure about what happened," the student asserted.

"Bekka," Ms. McDowell directed, "please come to my desk and bring your purse. Let's make absolutely sure your fifty dollars didn't slide into some crevice in your purse."

"No need to do that ma'am, 'cause I've been robbed," Bekka said sadly. "Just like them other girls."

"Just humor me, Bekka," Ms. McDowell said, "and bring your purse to my desk. Sometimes we're sure of something and it turns out we're mistaken. I'm always putting things in the wrong places in my purse."

Bekka walked slowly up to the teacher's desk. Ms. McDowell took a newspaper from her briefcase and spread it on the top of her desk. Then she explained, "When I lose something in my purse, I just upend it and spill everything out." With that, she spilled the contents of Bekka's purse onto her desktop.

"See," Bekka sighed, "just a few old dollars spilled from my wallet. The fifty is gone."

Ms. McDowell sorted through lipsticks, mirrors, packets of sugar and creamer, little booklets, and packets of tissues.

"See it ain't anywhere," Bekka repeated.

"What's this little purse here?" Ms. McDowell asked.

"Oh, that's for my lip balm, ma'am . . . chapped lips you know. I keep my lip balm in there," Bekka replied.

"Well," Ms. McDowell said, opening the little purse. "We'll just take a quick peek in here and—eureka! We've found it. Look, a fifty dollar bill folded into a tight little cylinder right next to your lip balm."

"Oh my gosh," Bekka gasped. "How on earth did that happen? What was I thinking? I was sure I put the money in my wallet. I must've put it in there by mistake. Stupid me! I'm so sorry for causing such a fuss, Ms. McDowell."

Alonee glanced over at Jaris. Her eyebrows shot up. Bekka was trying to fake being the victim of a theft.

"I think this is a good time for a little lecture not directly related to our course of study," Ms. McDowell began, once Bekka was back in her seat. "There have apparently been some thefts from purses here at school, and proceeds from the cheerleader car wash is missing. Events like that can foster hysteria and mistrust, which is sad. Some people might even use the situation to pretend money was taken when it was not. If the money is from parents, often their mom and dad will replace it. Then the culprit has twice as much money. We don't want that to happen."

"Oh," Bekka exclaimed, "that would be terrible to fake such a thing."

"Indeed," Ms. McDowell agreed.

The teacher then began passing out the corrected class projects. Jaris held his breath. He'd worked very hard on his project, but maybe he could have done even better if he wasn't so worried about Sereeta. When Ms. McDowell put the folder on the edge of his desk, Jaris was afraid to look at the grade. How much was his tardiness going to cost him? Then he took a deep breath and looked.

A minus! Jaris heaved a deep sigh of relief. McDowell had taken off only part of a point for being late.

After class, Jaris saw Bekka arguing with another girl. "I told you it wouldn't work," Bekka hissed. "Now the teacher thinks I'm a cheat. She knows what I did. And it's all your fault!"

Jaris heard just one more phrase. This came from the lips of the other girl.

"It worked for Ryann."

Jaris felt rage pulsing through his body. The first "theft" had been a ruse from the beginning—greedy little teenagers wanting to squeeze more money from their parents by pretending they had been robbed. The words ran through Jaris's mind again and again. "It worked for Ryann. . . . It worked for Ryann." All the ugliness, all the suspicions, and all the accusations—innocent people suffered through all that.

At lunchtime, Jaris looked for Ryann and Leticia. They always found a little corner to eat in. Jaris spotted them, noticing that Ryann was sporting a new tank top with alternating bright white and black stripes. "Hi Ryann, did you ever find that hundred dollars that was missing from your purse?" Jaris asked.

"Of course not," Ryann answered. "Some thief took it."

Leticia glared at Jaris and said, "What a stupid question. You know what happened."

"Yeah," Jaris said. "I know exactly what happened. A couple girls spilled the beans." Jaris looked directly into Ryann's eyes and spoke in a clear, harsh voice. "Ryann, *I know what you did*. I know what you did standing there in front of Harriet Tubman's statue. You should be ashamed to stand by the statue of a good, honest, brave woman like Harriet Tubman and run a dirty con job like you did."

Ryann jumped up, looking frightened. "W-what are you talking about?" she stammered. "I don't know what you're talking about. I didn't do anything."

"Ryann, shhh," Leticia cautioned. "Don't say anything!"

Jaris turned and looked at Leticia. "Were you the brains behind the little scam? You know it's bad enough to lie about something like that, to deliberately trick people into believing you've been robbed of a hundred dollars. But it's even worse to cast suspicion on an innocent person. That's pure evil."

Leticia grabbed Ryann's hand. Ryann was shaking. "He doesn't know what he's talking about," Leticia said to her. "He's just guessing. He doesn't know anything. Don't panic, girl."

"You wanted to buy more than a hundred dollars worth of rags, girl," Jaris continued. "So you came up with a way to double your fun, and you didn't care who got hurt."

"It's all lies," Ryann asserted, clamping her hands over her ears. "I won't listen to no more lies."

"Then your cousin Liza caught on to the scam and tried to double her money too," Jaris went on.

Jaris dropped to one knee in the grass and stared at both girls. "Listen up and listen good. You're going to tell your parents that you found the hundred dollars you thought was stolen. I don't care what kind of story you cook up, but you're going to fess up to finding the money. The whole school is going to know it was a mistake, that Sereeta didn't take your freakin' money. Nobody did. I know you tried to cheat your parents, but that's not my business. I'm giving you guys a way out so you don't have to admit to the crooks you are. Pass the word to your cousin too."

"He can't make you do anything," Leticia said. "He's just blowin' smoke, Ryann. You get out of our faces, Jaris Spain. You don't scare us!"

"Fine," Jaris said. "After school today I'm going over to your house, Ryann, and tell your parents what you did. Then I'm telling Liza's parents what she did."

"They w-won't believe you," Ryann gasped.

"Don't let him scare you," Leticia urged. "Don't let that creep scare you."

"Wanna bet they won't believe me?" Jaris sneered. "I bet over the past two weeks you've spent a lot more than a hundred dollars on new tops and jeans. All your parents have to do is look in your closet. They'll get the picture. I got a feeling girl, if you did something this underhanded, you've stepped over the line before. Your parents won't be all that surprised, but this time they'll come down on you like a ton of bricks. Count on it. You tell everybody, including the school office, that you found the money and it wasn't stolen after all. Or you're in deep trouble."

Jaris got up and brushed the grass from the knee of his jeans. "Hop to it, girl," he commanded her. "If I don't hear something before the last bell today, you can see me at your house tonight. I'm not kidding."

"He can't do this to you," Leticia protested, but her voice lacked conviction now. Ryann began to sob wildly.

About an hour before the end of the school day, Alonee told Jaris she saw Ryann and Liza Ann in the principal's office. Ryann was crying. Jaris figured the school officials knew the girls were not being truthful about finding the money and weren't coming clean out of the goodness of their hearts. But they would accept the story. The girls weren't criminals. Nobody, including Jaris, wanted their reputations to be trashed.

That wouldn't do anybody any good. The wisest choice was just to accept a dubious story from two little con artists and clear everybody of stealing.

Jaris expected the matter would be put to rest in the morning with an announcement from the principal. But there was still the question of what happened to the missing car wash money. After school, Jaris climbed on his motorcycle and rode to the Pierce home. When he arrived at the small rental house, he was shocked by its disrepair. The screens were torn, and the screen door hung on one hinge. A rusted old air conditioner teetered precariously from a window sill. Quincy had said his family was hard up, but Jaris never expected anything this bad. He felt sorry for the family. But he needed to clear Sereeta.

When Jaris pushed the doorbell, nothing happened. It too was broken. He banged on the door with his hand.

Suzy Pierce appeared in the doorway. "Hello," she said. "You're too young to be a bill collector, so what do you want here?"

"I'm Jaris Spain. I'm a junior at Tubman High like your son," Jaris replied.

"Oh, well Quincy isn't home," Mrs. Pierce said wearily. "He's out looking for work. Lord knows we need the money."

"May I talk to you about something, Mrs. Pierce?" Jaris asked. He felt sorry for the woman. She probably wasn't much older than Jaris's mother, but she looked far older. She'd led a hard life, and it had taken its toll. There was nothing left of her youth. She was overweight. Fattening, less nutritious food was cheaper than healthful fruits, vegetables, and lean meats. When you can't pay your bills, you spend less time worrying about balanced diets and good foods.

"Can we just sit here on the steps?" Mrs. Pierce suggested. "I'd ask you inside, but the house is a mess. It's always a mess. I work like a dog keeping the hospital clean, and I got nothing left for my own house. I'm just so tired. My husband is ill, you know. He can't help with nothin'."

101

"Yeah, I'm sorry, Mrs. Pierce," Jaris said and waited a second before going on. "You know all about the money missing from the Saturday car wash."

Mrs. Pierce's face clouded over in misery. "Yeah, I'm so sorry I got mixed up in that. It was a big mess like most everything in my life," she sighed.

"This girl who helped you sort the bills, Sereeta Prince," Jaris asked gently. "Were you there all the time she was sorting?"

"Yeah, I was right beside her. She's a smart girl," Mrs. Pierce replied.

"They're hinting that she might have taken some of the money, and she's really heartbroken because she's an honest person," Jaris continued. "She's a close friend of mine, and I'm trying to get to the bottom of what happened to that two hundred dollars."

"Oh, she didn't take anything," Mrs. Pierce asserted. "I told them that when the school people talked to me. She's a dear, sweet little thing. Who's saying terrible things about her?"

"Some of the kids," Jaris answered. "And your son sort of said that maybe Sereeta took some of the money. He was really upset about you getting in trouble, and that's why he said it. He didn't mean to cause trouble for Sereeta. He was afraid the school might blame you and want you guys to come up with the missing two hundred dollars."

Mrs. Pierce shrank back in horror. "Oh, I couldn't!" she cried. "I couldn't come up with two hundred dollars. I couldn't come up with anything. We've got medical bills piled up in there. More come in every day. My husband didn't have medical insurance on his job. When he got sick, all the bills came to us . . . big bills . . . scary numbers. The lady at the hospital is helpin' us get the Medicaid, but in the meantime the bills just keep comin' in. Summa them doctors want thousands of dollars! I wake up every morning with a headache. I'm terrified."

"I'm really sorry," Jaris sympathized. "I just wanted to know if you could say for sure that Sereeta didn't take any money from the cash box."

"I'm sure she didn't," Mrs. Pierce replied, then sounded unsure. "But it was all so confusing. Anything could have happened. I never should have volunteered for that. It was all such a mess." Tears rolled down her weathered face. "I'm just at the end of my rope."

"It's okay, Mrs. Pierce," Jaris assured her. "Thanks for talking with me. I hope things get better for you." Jaris hurried back to his motorcycle, knowing no more than when he came.

On Thursday morning at Tubman High, the principal came on the PA system to make the announcement Jaris was hoping for:

Students, we have very good news. Of late there has been an apparent rash of thefts from girls' purses. We are now gratified to inform the students here at Tubman High that both girls who believed they were victims of theft have now located the missing money. We wish to thank the students who came forward with this information. This does not mean we shouldn't continue to be vigilant at all times about guarding our valuables. Never leave your purses or wallets unattended. Thefts can occur, and we all have the responsibility to protect ourselves with prudence and wisdom. But we are happy to let you know that these particular instances of lost money were the result of errors, not theft.

"What do you make of that?" Jasmine asked Marko during the few minutes before class began. "Those fool girls thought their money was stolen, and now they found it?"

"Sounds like bull to me," Marko remarked.

Jaris sat nearby but said nothing. He would never say anything about what he knew. Ryann and Liza's misdeeds were, to him, dead issues. He had promised them that if they repaired the damage they did, he would keep quiet. He meant to keep that promise.

The announcement deeply relieved Jaris. He felt a little lighthearted as he headed for his midmorning English class. But just before he entered the building, he noticed a car coming into the visitor's parking area at an unsafe speed. It was weaving from side to side as well. At first he thought somebody was losing control, but then he realized there was something wrong with the driver. The car came to a stop, taking up two spaces. The driver started to get out, losing a shoe in the process. She retrieved her shoe, almost losing her balance. She wore a green sweater and pajama bottoms. She was a pretty woman who looked very drunk.

Jaris caught his breath, his heart sinking.

It was Sereeta's mother.

Other students noticed the woman too and gathered into small groups. Some laughed, and some looked concerned that she would hurt herself.

"Look, something's wrong with that lady," a boy remarked. "She can't hardly walk."

"Somebody needs to help her," a girl added.

Mr. Pippin was just arriving, his battered briefcase bulging with corrected test papers. Whenever he walked from the faculty parking area, he usually looked straight ahead, never to the side. He was always afraid he would see something that would require his attention as a teacher—a fight, an argument, somebody in trouble. He didn't want to get involved in anything. He just wanted to get to the classroom quickly, teach his class, and go home.

But the woman fell to her knees as Jaris and two other students were running toward her. She let out a small cry, like a wounded cat.

"Good grief!" Mr. Pippin said in exasperation. "What is that now?" He was the only teacher around, and he was forced to go over to her to help.

"Madam, are you all right?" Mr. Pippin asked, as Jaris and another boy helped her to her feet.

"I am quite all right," Mrs. Manley said in the precise voice of people who are drunk and know it and who wish to speak clearly to hide their condition.

"Look," Marko Lane howled. "It's Sereeta's mom. She's drunk as a skunk! Look at her! Old Pippin is trying to hold her up!"

Jaris was sick to his stomach. He couldn't believe this was happening.

"Well thank you, Jack," Mrs. Manley said to Jaris. "Thank you very much. I am perfectly fine, but somehow I t-tripped." She looked at Mr. Pippin and tried to smile. "Is this your grandfather, Jack? What a nice gentleman."

"No, this is Mr. Pippin, our English teacher," Jaris replied. He glanced in anguish at the growing crowd of students. He hadn't seen Sereeta at school, but he hoped against hope that she wasn't nearby to see this scene.

"I have come," Mrs. Manley announced, "on b-behalf of my daughter . . . to p-protest the sander—slanderous accusations made against her!"

Mr. Pippin had begun to wave his arms threateningly to shoo away the mob of students who'd come to see the show.

CHAPTER SEVEN

"Go to your classes at once," Mr. Pippin screamed. "Go! Do you hear me? Go!" There is nothing to see here."

He was having no luck until Ms. McDowell and the vice principal, Mr. Hawthorne, came along.

"All students will disperse immediately and go to their classes or face detention!" Mr. Hawthorne shouted.

"Everybody . . . right away!" Ms. McDowell added, sending most of the students on their way.

Ms. McDowell came forward and laid a comforting hand on Olivia Manley's arm. "Are you all right?" she asked.

"I am ex-cell-ent," the woman declared, her eyes fixed on Mr. Hawthorne. "Are you the principal, sir?"

"I'm the vice principal," he replied.

"Well," Mrs. Manley began her speech, "the people in this school—these people— they are spreading lies about my daughter. And I am in-incensed! And I want it to be stopped."

Jaris and a few other students remained nearby.

"Please," Jaris begged, "take her inside." He kept glancing around for Sereeta. With any luck, she'd stayed home with the baby.

"Come along with us, Jack," Mrs. Manley commanded, reaching for Jaris's hand. "I know you are Sereeta's friend . . . you can tell these people what has been going on."

Mr. Hawthorne, Ms. McDowell, Jaris, and Mrs. Manley marched toward the administration building. Inside the building, they all disappeared into the vice principal's office. As soon as the office door was closed behind them, Mr. Hawthorne turned immediately to Jaris. "Do you know what this is about?" he asked.

"Yeah," Jaris explained, "you know the thing about the girls' purses being robbed? Well, that got cleared up this morning. So that's out of the way. But then there's this missing money from the cheerleader car wash. Some kids who don't like Sereeta— this lady's daughter—they've been spreading nasty rumors, saying Sereeta was involved in the thefts."

"My husband got very angry. Very, very angry," Mrs. Manley announced. "It got to his . . . his b-business ass-associates that his stepdaughter was involved in nef-ar-ious activity. We had a terrible argument . . . for days we argued. I want this stopped at once."

"Well, Mrs. Manley," Mr. Hawthorne responded, "we are very sorry about all this. We here at Tubman respect Sereeta

Prince as a fine student and a wonderful young lady. There was never any intention of implying that she did anything dishonest. When the PE department talked to her, they were just looking for her help in the inquiry into the missing car wash funds. I assure you, we all hold Sereeta in high esteem. Now, the best thing for you to do at the moment is to go home. You are . . . ah . . . not in the best of health right now."

"I can do that," Mrs. Manley declared. "I can c-certainly do that." She fished in her purse for her keys. When she found them, she dropped them on the floor and almost toppled over trying to retrieve them. She made a short little laugh that sounded more like a gasp. "There now, we are all set. Jack, would you be kind enough to help me to the parking lot where my car is?"

"Mrs. Manley," Mr. Hawthorne said quickly. "I'll drive you home."

"I'll follow you in my car and bring you back to the school," Ms. McDowell volunteered.

"And just why is that? I cannot see why that is," Mrs. Manley insisted. "I am p-perfectly capable of driving my own car home."

"You're not well, Mrs. Manley," Mr. Hawthorne said in an aggrieved voice.

Ms. McDowell turned to Jaris. "Jaris, go to my classroom and tell them I'll be there in twenty minutes. In the meantime, put on the video of President Clinton's press conference. We'll discuss it when I return."

Jaris hurried to American history. His legs felt like they didn't want to carry him. He kept thinking, "Poor Sereeta, poor Sereeta. If she's here on campus, it'll be terrible. Even if she isn't, everybody'll be talking about her mom."

Jaris glanced back and saw Mr. Hawthorne helping Sereeta's mother into the passenger side of her car. She was loudly protesting, but eventually he got her to get in. Soon the two cars vanished down the street.

When Jaris got into the classroom, word had already spread about what happened.

"Hey, Sereeta's mom was one drunken lady," Marko cried, setting off a burst of laughter.

"You should a seen old Pippin trying to get her up," a girl laughed.

Jaris raced to get the video started. He turned to the class, "Ms. McDowell wants us to watch President Clinton's press conference from back in 1993, and she said there might be a test on it. So shut up and take notes." He added the part about the test. He was desperate to bring the class to order and make them stop ridiculing poor Mrs. Manley. For the first time in his life, Jaris knew exactly what poor Mr. Pippin felt like every time he had to face these people.

Ms. McDowell returned twenty-four minutes later. She walked in briskly, saying nothing about the events of the morning. She immediately launched into a comparison of President Clinton's press conference style with those of John F. Kennedy and Richard M. Nixon. Ms. McDowell acted as if nothing unusual had happened. When the class ended, she asked Jaris, "Could you remain for a moment?"

"Sure," Jaris complied. He took a seat near the teacher's desk.

When the room was empty, she sat at the desk and began speaking to him. "Jaris, thank you for handling the class for me. There are very few students I would entrust with that responsibility. You're a special young man. But that's not what I need to say to you.

"I know you and Sereeta are close friends, and I can't think of many things worse for a teenager than what happened this morning. Tell Sereeta to come and talk to me. But before she does, will you tell her this for me? I am thirty-one years old, and every morning when I wake up, I feel blessed to have the life I do. But until I was twenty, my life was a train wreck. Worse things happened to me than what happened today. Much worse. You hurt and you bleed, but then you heal. And you are stronger in the scarred places than you thought you ever could be. You tell Sereeta it's going to be okay. She's a bright, compassionate, wonderful girl full of potential. Tell her to hang in there." Ms. McDowell was done with what she had to say, but Jaris waited a moment.

"Thank you," he then said, "I will."

Later in the day, Sami Archer told Jaris that she hadn't seen Sereeta in any of her classes. At his next break between classes, Jaris called Sereeta.

"Sereeta. You okay?" Jaris asked her. He didn't know if he should mention what happened at school. Surely Ms. McDowell and Mr. Hawthorne had been there by the time he had a chance to call, Jaris thought.

"Yes," she answered. "A nanny just came. She's starting full-time tomorrow but she's getting used to everything today. She'll be with the baby all the time from now on." Sereeta sounded strange to Jaris. She didn't sound frightened, or upset, or sad, or *anything*. She sounded like a robot.

"See you in school tomorrow, then, huh Sereeta?" Jaris asked.

"Yes," she replied.

"Uh . . . should I come over after school or something? If you'd like I could . . . I mean, we could talk," Jaris suggested.

"No, it's all right," Sereeta said. "See you tomorrow."

When the call ended, Jaris was sorry he didn't give Sereeta the message from Ms. McDowell. But the time just didn't seem right.

After school, as Jaris walked up the driveway at home, his mother came outside. "Have you talked to Sereeta, Jaris?" she asked.

"Yeah, I spoke with her today," Jaris said.

"Is she okay? Alonee's mom called me and told me what happened. Thank God Sereeta wasn't in school today," Mom declared.

"I don't know if she's okay or not, Mom," Jaris remarked. "She didn't say much. She was sorta like a zombie."

"Poor Olivia," Mom commented. "She really seems to be going downhill. I keep wondering if there was something more I could have done when she and Tom were breaking up. Tom isn't a bad man. He seemed to be good for Olivia. Maybe if I'd talked to her more . . . I mean, your father and I have had our rocky places . . . but we fought for our marriage. It's worth fighting for, it really is." Mom looked intently at Jaris and asked, "Was it awful at school? I mean was she . . . did you see her?"

"Yeah , it wasn't good," Jaris answered. He felt bad even talking about it. Mrs. Manley was Sereeta's *mother*. When all was said and done, she was the mother of the girl Jaris loved. Whatever flaws she had, nothing could change that. It seemed disloyal to go into the details—how Mr. Pippin acted, how Mrs. Manley fell. "Mom," he signed, "it just makes me so sick I can't talk about it."

"I understand, sweetie," Mom said.

When Sereeta came into American history the next morning, Jaris started talking to her about the announcement the day

119

before. "There never was any money taken from those purses," he told her. "The girls found their freakin' money laying around, so that's settled anyway."

Before Ms. McDowell arrived, Jaris saw other students whispering and snickering. Marko and Jasmine nudged each other as they looked at Sereeta. But when Ms. McDowell appeared, there was perfect order as usual.

At the break, Jaris and Sereeta went to the vending machine. He bought a big red apple. He smiled at Sereeta and asked, "Do you remember when you told me their official name was Delicious?"

"I remember," Sereeta responded but wanted to talk about something else. "Mom said you helped her yesterday. She said you were very nice. She's still calling you Jack, but I knew who she meant."

"She okay today?" Jaris asked, focusing on his apple.

"Yeah. She has a terrible headache," Sereeta said. Sereeta peeled her orange. "It was pretty awful, wasn't it? Yesterday, I mean."

"No, not awful . . . just . . . you know," Jaris struggled.

"Awful," Sereeta affirmed. "I suppose the usual suspects were laughing at her."

"Well, Ms. McDowell and Mr. Hawthorne showed up pretty fast, and they got everybody back to class," Jaris reported.

"See, they'd been arguing for days, Mom and Perry," Sereeta explained. "About my character of all things. Perry was all bent out of shape. He's in banking and stuff, and he was thinking having a notorious criminal like me for a stepdaughter might damage his image. With all the financial scandals in the news, he thought people would think I was ripping off Tubman High School and he was cheating his clients. So he was ragging on Mom. 'What kind of a daughter did you raise?' Mom doesn't usually defend me. But when she's up against the wall, she drinks, and the liquor makes her brave enough to do stuff she wouldn't usually do. So off she marches to Tubman High like a knight on a white horse to rescue my reputation . . . poor Mom. The only noble thing she's tried to do for me, and it ends up making a mockery of her . . . and of me. What's that saying? You can't win for losing."

"It'll be okay," Jaris assured her. "You know something? Ms. McDowell said some really nice things about you. She said she'd like to talk to you sometime."

"What would we talk about?" Sereeta asked, tossing her orange peel into the trash.

"Oh," Jaris paused to think of the right words. "She's had some experiences that she'd like to share with you. Sometimes it helps to hear how other people have dealt with . . . you know, stuff."

"I'm the sad case now, aren't I?" Sereeta commented bitterly. "I'm poor Sereeta. Look at her. She's always crying about stuff going on in her life. Then she's accused of being a thief. And now her mom comes to school drunk and makes a fool of herself . . . my friends act real cheerful like nothing happened, but you can see it in their eyes. 'Poor Sereeta . . . shhh, here she comes, poor thing.' Quick, talk about that new comedy at the movie theater . . ."

"Don't get paranoid, girl," Jaris said. "The truth is most of us got so much trash going on in our lives that we don't know or care about somebody else's trash. Like Quincy. I was over at his house the other day and it's a mess. The family is struggling with heaps of bills, and everything at the house is broken."

"What were you doing over there, Jaris?" Sereeta asked.

"I just wanted to talk to Mrs. Pierce about that car wash money," Jaris explained. "How two hundred dollars disappeared like that. I guess things were pretty messed up with bills floating around."

"I suppose they still think I dipped in and took some bills when I helped Mrs. Pierce sort the money out," Sereeta said.

"I don't think so," Jaris answered. "I think when those girls found the money that was supposed to be stolen from their purses, it sort of took the heat outta this whole theft scare. A lot of kids are thinking now maybe something like that happened at the car wash. Somebody just made a big mistake. Or maybe the money just blew away. Who knows? It was a windy day."

The bell rang and they went to English.

Mr. Pippin seemed to do a double take on Sereeta when she came in. Jaris thought maybe he only imagined the reaction, but was Mr. Pippin wondering how such a nice girl could have a mother like that? Were a lot of the kids thinking the same thing? Jaris felt protective of Sereeta. He wished he could build a wall around her or raise a curtain to protect her from the stares and snickers. Everytime students seemed to be looking in Sereeta's direction, Jaris figured they were judging her, and he was angry. He didn't like being so obsessed. He told Sereeta to just ignore everything, and he wanted to do the same himself. But he couldn't always.

After class, Sereeta and Jaris were walking across the campus when a boy Jaris hardly knew, Kyle Samson, stopped and spoke to Sereeta. "Is your mother like that all the time? I saw her at school yesterday, and she was falling-down drunk, and I wondered if she was drunk all the time?"

Jaris turned to the boy and grabbed a fistful of his shirt. He gave him a hard shake and yelled in his face. "Haven't you got anything better to do than bother people, jerk?" Jaris couldn't believe he'd lost it so completely in just a split second. The boy turned and sprinted away, obviously frightened.

"Jaris," Sereeta cried, "don't do stuff like that!"

"Where'd he come off asking a stupid, idiotic question like that?" Jaris stormed. "He doesn't even know you. What a stupid jerk! I should have decked him, that's what I should have done."

Jaris looked around him. A lot of students were walking on the campus. Some seemed to be looking in the direction of Sereeta and Jaris—and laughing. Jaris thought most of them were laughing about Sereeta's mother. But maybe they were laughing about something else. Jaris felt strange, as though he were alone in the world with Sereeta. All around them were enemies, and they were laughing and jeering and trying to hurt her. And their ridicule was almost killing Jaris.

Jaris wanted to grab Sereeta's hand and run with her to some secret place where nobody knew them, where they could be together in peace. But there was no secret place. There was just Tubman High School and all the laughing faces that eventually morphed before Jaris's eyes into one big laughing face.

Then, suddenly, there was Derrick Shaw, his wide, almost handsome face twisted in mirth. He was doubled over in laughter, clutching at his stomach as if he couldn't contain it. "Didja see—" he gasped between spasms of laugher. "Didja see—didja see . . . the big seagull? He was up there, flyin' up there just minding his own business, and he got a call of nature!" Derrick pointed south over to the football field. "Big seagull come flyin' over football practice and he . . . he . . . ." Derrick was laughing so hard he could hardly speak, but he finally got it out. "He took a dump—right on Marko's head! Right on his head. Oh man, Marko was so mad! He's runnin' with his fist in the air and he's yelling at the seagull, but the bird don't care . . . Didja see it, Jaris? Didja see it, Sereeta?"

"You're kidding!" Jaris exclaimed, starting to laugh himself.

"Wow," Sereeta giggled. "How'd the seagull know it was Marko? And they say birds are dumb."

Jaris felt as though a demon had been beating up his soul, and now it had been cast out. Now, he felt, his soul could heal.

Kevin Walker joined them, and he was laughing too. "You don't see many seagulls around here, but that dude had a job to do," he chuckled.

Derrick kept on laughing and trying to talk at the same time. "Marko, he's so mad . . . but the old seagull, he's on his way to the ocean. He been to the little boy's room!"

CHAPTER EIGHT

In American history the next morning—Thursday—Ms. McDowell made an announcement. "I have something special to talk about this morning before we start class. In three weeks, we'll be having a birthday celebration for the namesake of our school, Harriet Tubman. Now we know Harriet Tubman was born around 1820, but we don't know the exact date of her birth because she was a slave. Records of slave births and deaths were not kept in many cases. So we're just really guessing at her actual birth date. So the event will be in the school auditorium on a Friday night, and there'll be drama and music from the glee club. I need students who are good orators with a little acting experience, if possible. We'll need six students—one to play Harriet Tubman and five to take the roles of other slaves, those she led to freedom. If you'd like to be part of the program, let me know at the end of class."

Jaris glanced over at Sereeta. "You could be Harriet Tubman," he whispered. "You were so good in *A Tale of Two Cities* as Lucie."

Sereeta shook her head vigorously. "No," her lips formed the word.

Jaris was eager to be part of the program. He had a good strong voice, and everybody said he made a great Sydney Carton in the play. Jaris thought he could be an inspiring young slave crying out for freedom.

When the class ended, Jaris went to the desk to sign up for the auditions. He looked back at Sereeta. "Come on," he pleaded.

"No way," Sereeta said.

Ms. McDowell said, "You know what, Sereeta? When you started this class, I thought, 'Wow, this girl is me fifteen years ago. She's tough. She's spirited. She's got it.' You'd make a wonderful Harriet Tubman. I'd like for you to try out for the part."

Jasmine spoke up. "I'd like to try out too. I haven't acted, but I think I could do it."

"Fine, just sign up," Ms. McDowell urged her too.

Jaris took Sereeta's hand. He pulled her to the front of the room where the sign-up sheet was. "Do it for me," he told her.

Sereeta frowned and signed her name.

Ms. McDowell took down twelve names. "On Friday, after the last bell, we'll have a little audition right here in the classroom," she said. "I've passed out all the parts to you twelve, so you'll be ready to do your stuff."

As they left the classroom, Sereeta told Jaris, "I don't need this. I am so not up for this." Sereeta held up her hand in a gesture of protest.

"It'll make you feel better, Sereeta," Jaris assured her.

"Well, I'll do the dumb audition, but my heart's not in it," she sighed.

On Friday afternoon, the twelve students reported to Ms. McDowell's classroom. Only two girls signed up to try out for Harriett Tubman.

Jasmine went first. She read the words of Harriet Tubman when she became free: "I had crossed the line of which I had so long been dreaming. I was free." Jasmine shouted out the words, in anger and triumph. Her Harriet Tubman was a strident person, like Jasmine.

Then Sereeta got up to do her audition. Jaris looked at the slim girl, fear in her eyes. Sereeta didn't want to do this. She felt bad inside, still humiliated by what her mother had done at school. And some suspicion about the missing car wash money still hung over her head. But her feelings ran much deeper than those caused by humiliation or suspicion. Sereeta felt lonely and disregarded. She had read a little about Harriet

Tubman. Like Tubman, Sereeta was a young black woman, no family to rely on, alone in the world and fighting for her place in it.

Sereeta was raw emotionally. Her voice trembled as she spoke the words. "I had crossed the line of which I had so long been dreaming," she spoke the words with a tear in her voice. Then she summoned her courage and cried, "I was free!" Sereeta sat down then. The other students then auditioned for the roles of slaves rescued by Harriet Tubman. Jaris read the role of a slave led by Tubman through an icy river.

"We came to the water and there was no bridge," Jaris read. "We men didn't want to get into that cold water. Harriet Tubman got right in, with the water to her armpits. And she walked, and we followed, though we didn't know where we were going. We leaned on her and on our faith in God."

When everybody had finished reading, Ms. McDowell declared, "Good job everybody. Okay, we'll have a couple of rehearsals, and we need some of you for costume changes and scenes and other backup jobs. I'll tell you when. Now for the cast. As slaves led to freedom by Harriett Tubman, we have Kevin Walker, Derrick Shaw, Alonee Lennox, Marko Lane, and Jaris Spain. As Harriet Tubman—Sereeta Prince."

Sereeta looked at Jaris and rolled her eyes. "See what you got me into!" she hissed.

"It'll be fun," Jaris promised.

"Sereeta, have you a few minutes?" Ms. McDowell asked.

Sereeta shrugged. "I guess so." As Jaris left, Sereeta was pulling up a chair at the teacher's desk.

When Jaris went home, he rehearsed his part in the Harriet Tubman birthday tribute. He thought being on the stage again, and playing a part would be fun. He'd enjoy seeing his family and friends in the audience. The glee club from Tubman would sing many of the old spirituals that the slaves relied on for strength and used as a code in their travels through the night.

The next day, Jaris asked Sereeta if she had a nice talk with Ms. McDowell.

"Yeah," Sereeta enthused. "She told me I could share what she told me with anybody. Oh Jaris, I was blown away. Her parents both died of a drug overdose. There were five kids in the family, and only three survived to adulthood. It's like a miracle what she's made of herself."

"I knew she overcame a lot," Jaris replied, "but I didn't know it was that tough."

"She was a little kid in the projects," Sereeta went on to explain, "and both parents were doing crack cocaine. She met this lady, this old lady who was like a do-gooder or something. She reached out to kids with problems, and she helped Ms. McDowell get into college, and it made all the difference. They stayed friends until the lady died. Ms. McDowell said that woman was really her mother."

Jaris smiled at Sereeta. He could see that the talk with Ms. McDowell had done her some good. But then Sereeta added, "But Jaris, she's so strong. Ms. McDowell is so strong. I wish I truly was like that. But I fall apart so easily. I always want to give up . . ."

"You're strong, Sereeta," Jaris encouraged her. "Wanting to give up is okay. Actually giving up is bad, and you won't ever do that."

"Oh Jaris," Sereeta complained, "I get depressed and I do stupid things. I've never told you this before, and please never tell anybody, but do you know what I did once? It was just so bad at home it was like I didn't exist. So I went out to this field, you know, where the burned house is, and I . . . oh Jaris, you promise you'll never tell anybody if I tell you something horrible and disgusting?"

"I promise," Jaris said.

"I cut myself, Jaris," Sereeta confessed. "I was hurting so bad inside, that I took a sharp knife and I cut my arm three times. My arm hurt so much and it bled, but in a way it stopped the hurting inside me. I guess it hurt so much that I forgot how they didn't care about me and stuff. I was just so scared I'd bleed to death or something. And then I didn't even care if I did or not. Don't ever tell anybody, Jaris. It was so sick and disgusting."

"I won't tell, Sereeta," Jaris assured her, although he knew already. He knew for a long time, and he never told and he never would. "But you don't do stuff like that anymore. You're stronger than that now."

"If only I'd stop wanting her to be a mother," Sereeta confided. "I mean, why am I such a fool? She's never really been a mother. I could always tell she wasn't crazy about me. I mean, like you know some mothers are. Like your mom. She loves you and Chelsea so much. She looks at you guys like the sun and the moon rises on you. And Alonee's mom, and Sami's. You know what Alonee's mom said to her once? She said, 'Alonee, I love you more than my next breath.' Why can't I stop wanting what I'll never have?"

"She does the best she can, I guess," Jaris suggested.

"Yeah," Sereeta agreed. "She's not happy either. She thought she'd be happy with Perry, but it's not great. And she tried to be with the baby all the time, but then that went sour too. Now the nanny's taken over. Poor Jake. I hated him so much before he was born. He was like the dirty little guy who was taking my rightful place as the beloved child in the family. Now I feel sorry for him. He's not the beloved child either. There *is* no beloved child."

On Saturday, when Jaris got home from his job at the Chicken Shack, he saw a strange car in the driveway. He'd seen it before but he couldn't place it. When he went inside the house, he was startled to see Sereeta's mother. She smiled at Jaris and said, "Your mother called me and asked me if I'd like to go shopping with her like we did in the old days. Just up and called me. We got to talking and it was like old times, wasn't it, Monica?"

Jaris's mother nodded agreement. "Now Olivia and I are going shopping at the mall. Do you know how long it's been since we did that? You and Sereeta were about seven years old!"

"Yeah, we're hittin' the malls, boy," Mrs. Manley declared. "Going in the dressing rooms and laughing at each other when we try on dresses that are too small . . . why not, huh, Monica?"

"Uh, that's good," Jaris commented.

"Yeah, I think so," Sereeta's mother said.

"So, Jaris," Mom instructed him, "if I don't get home by dinnertime, maybe your father will make something or else there's plenty of frozen dinners." Mom grabbed her purse and headed for the door with Mrs. Manley at her side.

Chelsea waited until they were gone, then she said to Jaris, "Some of the kids at middle school got brothers and sisters at Tubman, and they were talking about her and the trouble she had."

"Yeah, well," Jaris replied, "maybe being with our mom will be good for her. It seems she was doing better in the old days when they were friends."

"Is Sereeta okay?" Chelsea asked.

"Yeah, she's hanging in there, chili pepper," Jaris told her.

"Did they ever find the car wash money?" Chelsea asked.

"No," Jaris answered, as he dropped his books on the end table. Then he saw the letter on the table. It was addressed to him in a girl's handwriting. "What's this?" he asked Chelsea, holding up the envelope.

"I don't know, Jare," Chelsea giggled. "Maybe you got a secret admirer."

Jaris tore the envelope open and took out the letter.

Dear Jaris, I know you care about Sereeta and she's being blamed for the missing car wash money. I think you should know something. Quincy Pierce was once arrested for stealing money from a cash register where he used to work. We don't know each other very well but kind of got to know each other on that camping trip we all went on. I know Sereeta is a good person and wouldn't steal anything. I don't want her blamed for something she didn't do. I guess I should have said this face-to-face, but I just couldn't. Please don't say who told you this. Destini

"What's it say?" Chelsea asked. "Is she a secret admirer, Jare?"

"No, it's just something about school," Jaris said. "It's not important."

"But it *is* important," Jaris thought.

If Quincy Pierce had stolen money from his job, he'd be a good suspect for the theft from the car wash cash box. He might have easily stepped alongside his mother and taken the cash. She wouldn't be watching her own son.

Jaris felt sorry for Mrs. Pierce and all her troubles, but he had to get to the truth.

After school on Monday, Jaris spotted Quincy walking to the bus stop. "Hey man, got a minute?" Jaris called out.

"Yeah, but I don't want to miss my bus," Quincy called back. "I'm starting a new job tonight."

"It'll just take a minute, man," Jaris said. "You know they're still wondering about who took that car wash money."

Quincy seemed uneasy. "I gotta go," he groaned. "I'll miss the bus."

"The bus doesn't come for five more minutes, Quincy," Jaris told him. "I want to ask you something. You ever busted for stealing money from a cash box?"

Quincy's eyes widened and his mouth twitched. "Where'd you hear that?" he asked.

"Somebody told me. Somebody who didn't want Sereeta to get blamed for something she didn't do," Jaris replied.

"Well . . . yeah, okay," Quincy admitted. "I ain't denying it. I worked at a restaurant a long time ago, and I took a little money from the till. The guy who owned the place made a big deal of it. He called the cops and I got busted. But it was my first offense, so I got probation."

"A long time ago?" Jaris asked. "You're sixteen now, man."

"Okay, so it was last year. So what?" Quincy protested. "Look, it has nothing to do with the car wash money. I got nothing to do with that."

"You were pretty anxious to throw the blame on Sereeta," Jaris pressed.

"I'm sorry for that. I just was worried about my mom," Quincy said. "Mom is going through hell with all those bill collectors. She don't need no more grief, dude. Just get off my back, okay? The bus is coming. I didn't take no freakin' money. Your girlfriend is going to be okay. Everybody's forgetting about the car wash money. Just let it go, man." There was desperation in Quincy's voice.

When Quincy got on the bus, Jaris turned to go and saw Destini standing nearby.

"Hi!" she said. "What did he say about it? About being arrested for robbing his boss?"

"He admitted it," Jaris told her. "But he said he didn't take the car wash money. . . . You're Destini, right? I've seen you hanging out with Derrick."

"Yeah," Destini explained. "I belong to the church club that helps foster kids. That's where I met you and Sereeta." Jaris remembered her now. "Sereeta, she's really cool," Destini went on. "She's got a lot of heart. It burned me up when they were talking trash about her. I got nothing against Quincy. He's not a bad guy. But I found out he had a record and I thought maybe you should know. Quincy's mom and my mom work at the same hospital. Mrs. Pierce is a hard-luck lady. I feel sorry for them. But, you know, I don't want Sereeta blamed when she didn't do anything. I wanted to do the right thing. But I just couldn't get the courage to come up to you in person. And I didn't want word getting back to Quincy and his mom."

"Well, thank you for telling me," Jaris said gratefully.

"Please don't ever tell Quincy I ratted him out. I don't want any trouble, okay?" Destini pleaded.

"You got my word, girl," Jaris assured her. He watched Destini walk away. She seemed to be cautious around guys for some reason. Jaris figured she must have had a bad experience in her life with a boy and now she was gun-shy.

Jaris didn't know what to do with the information he had on Quincy. The guy screwed up last year, but that didn't mean he took the car wash money. Jaris hated the idea of never letting people forget their past. Still, Jaris didn't know where to go from here.

CHAPTER NINE

On the next day—Friday—around lunch-time at Tubman, Alonee pointed and said, "Look, Jaris. Isn't that Jasmine's parents going into the principal's office? I've never seen them coming around except at open house or something."

"Yeah," Jaris said, looking at the slim, attractive woman in an ivory-colored suit, and her equally trim and athletic husband. "I wonder what important business brings them here in the middle of the day. He must have taken time off from work."

Alonee laughed. "Maybe Jasmine got in another catfight with somebody, and the school called them in," she suggested. "I saw Jasmine this morning, and she seemed worried about something."

"You know, Jaris," Trevor added, "my mom goes to church with one of the ladies who work in the school office. Maybe this has nothing to do with them showing up, but Jasmine's mom has been sending emails back and forth with the PE department about the figures she turned in for the car wash. My mom's friend said they came across some mistakes that were made. Maybe it's nothing but . . ."

"Oh yeah?" Jaris responded with interest. "Jasmine has been making fun of Mrs. Pierce, saying she was too stupid to take care of the money at the car wash. Wouldn't it be something if it was Jasmine's mom who messed up?"

They all went to their classes then, and Jaris didn't think any more about it until he got to English class. Jasmine was in an animated discussion with several students about air-conditioning units.

"That's great, Jaz," one of the girls said. "It's really miserable in some of those classrooms with the old air conditioners. I mean they just don't work hard enough to cool the rooms on really hot days."

"Yeah," Jasmine affirmed. "My parents want to help Tubman High, so they're making a donation to get the air conditioners up-to-date in those rooms. This is my school after all. It'll be my alma mater. My parents are proud of Tubman and proud of me for doing so good."

"I saw your mom and dad going in the principal's office this morning," Jaris remarked.

"So what?" Jasmine asked sharply. "What business is it of yours if my parents are talking to the principal? You tell me that." Jasmine sounded defensive.

"I was just going to say—" Jaris started again.

"It's none of your business, Jaris Spain," Jasmine snapped. "You like to stick your nose in everything, but there's plenty you don't know about, and you got no business knowing. My parents are really good people, and they're respected by everybody in the community."

Jaris couldn't believe how defensive Jasmine was being. Now he was really suspicious. Maybe Trevor's mom was on to something—that Jasmine's mother was the one responsible for the missing two hundred dollars.

After school, Trevor talked to Jaris again. "Man, you know what I'm hearing? Jasmine's mom took the first shift at the car wash that Saturday, right? She kept tabs on the money that was turned in. Well, Jasmine's mom turned the cash box over to Mrs. Pierce and wrote down that there was four hundred and two dollars in the box. But Mrs. Pierce said there was two hundred and four dollars. Every time a car was washed, the kid taking the money from the car driver wrote up a slip. When the cheerleading coach and phys ed coach added up all the slips, they found out there was just two hundred and four dollars worth of car washes when Jasmine's mom went off duty."

"So Jasmine's mom mixed up the numbers," Jaris said.

Alonee joined the discussion. "Wow! All the abuse that Marko Lane has been heaping on Mrs. Pierce . . . all the crummy accusations against Sereeta. And maybe it all comes down to Jasmine's mom making an honest mistake?"

"Yeah," Jaris commented, "but can you see the school coming out and saying this whole mess was the result of even an easy mistake by this high-class lady—Lee Ann Benson?" Jaris posed a little dramatically as he said the name.

"So what happens?" Alonee asked. "A big coverup?"

"I think it has to do with air conditioners," Trevor suggested. "They'll invent this lie to explain the error. To save Mrs. Benson's reputation, the Bensons are donating new air-conditioning equipment to the school. Don't you see? It's a win-win situation. Jasmine's mom, the elegant Lee Ann Benson, comes off smelling like a rose. The school gets some free stuff, which is great at a time when they're axing school budgets all over town."

"And nobody will know what happened?" Jaris fumed. "A big cloud of mystery will continue to hang over the missing money?"

"We'll see," Trevor said.

In the morning they had their answer.

The principal made an announcement over the PA system:

Good morning, students. After an exhaustive examination of the cheerleader car wash receipts, we have discovered that a computer accounting error was made. The missing two hundred dollars was on paper, but never existed in reality. We regret this error and the distress it caused for so many of our students. We especially regret that the incident reflected on the honesty of so many good people when nothing wrong had taken place. In a gracious effort to turn this unfortunate event into a positive one, two of our hardworking parents, Lee Ann and Clyde Benson, parents of Tubman High junior Jasmine Benson, are donating money to renew the air-conditioning units in several of our classrooms, and for this we wish to thank them.

"Computer error! What a crock!" Jaris snarled when he and his friends gathered at the beverage machine. "Jasmine's mother screwed up, and she and her husband turn out the heroes."

"Yeah," Trevor agreed, "she made a rookie mistake, calling two hundred and four, four hundred and two. And Mrs. Pierce and Sereeta had to take the heat for it. And Jasmine's mom isn't even standing up and saying she's sorry."

"They're big shots," Alonee noted. "That's how big shots get through life. No use in griping about it. When little guys mess up, there's the devil to pay. When big shots mess up, everybody wants to smooth it over."

"Well," Jaris added, "at least the heat's off Sereeta and the Pierces. That's something."

All that day, the school buzzed with talk about the missing money and the donation.

Jasmine was very quiet in her afternoon classes. She sensed a lot of suspicion about the connection between her parents' donation and the mixup with the car wash money. Many of the kids were putting two and two together.

Between classes, Quincy approached her. "So I guess your mom messed up the till, not mine," he said bitterly. "And your boyfriend was going around calling my mom stupid."

"Where you get that?" Jasmine snarled. "That's crazy. Has nothing to do with anything. My parents just wanted to do something nice for the school 'cause there's been so much trouble and bad feelings. You oughta be thankful to them for doing it instead of thinking up stupid things."

"Yeah, right," Quincy remarked. "Your mom and dad just got the idea of making a donation when the school finally figured out there was an error at the car wash till."

"The computer did it," Jasmine snapped, "and if you don't shut your mouth, Quincy Pierce, you're going to have more trouble than you ever thought."

Another girl overheard the conversation and laughed. "Sure, blame it on the computer. I'm just wondering if your mom didn't rip off the cheerleaders, and now she's making up for it with the air conditioners."

"You take that back or I'll rip your eyelashes out, girl," Jasmine yelled.

Later, at lunch with Alonee and Destini, Sami Archer told them, "Good to see that trash-talking Jasmine off her high horse. She always so high and mighty. Now she gets to feel like some of the other kids when folks bad-mouth them. She always going on like her folks are better than my folks. She goes, 'Oh, your daddy is a garbage collector. Well, I guess that somebody has to do dirty jobs like that, but I'm sure glad *my* father works in a nice office and wears a suit.' "

And the buzz continued even after the last bell. Jaris told his parents what happened at school. "The official word that they're giving out is that some computer messed up the cheerleaders' car wash totals. But there's a lot of buzz that Jasmine's mom transposed some numbers and started the whole mess. Now Jasmine's parents are making a donation to the school, and I guess that means we'll never get the whole story."

"And that poor little girl—Sereeta—she had to go through all that garbage for no good reason," Pop said in an angry voice. "Well, too bad for her. Too bad for that Pierce lady too. I wonder who's giving them anything to make up for all that grief? Well, it is what it is, right? Like with me when I was a youngster thinking I was in line for a sports scholarship. Some bozo fouls me, crashes into me, and makes spaghetti out of my leg. But I'm a kid from the projects and he's from a ritzy family, and he didn't mean to foul me. Anyway, what's the big deal? I wasn't important. So what about my college dreams? I was a dumb kid from the projects, and I'd probably not been able to hack college anyway. So what's the difference if the bozo messed me up?"

Mom rolled her eyes. Pop was at it again, linking any injustice he heard about with his own personal misfortune. Pop was in another bad mood. It had not gone well at Jackson's. Too many beaters and not enough time. His back hurt. His feet hurt. His dreams of a better life were drifting farther and farther away, and he tore off the pages of the calendar. Though he ever really expected to reclaim his dream, it was rapidly getting too late even for fantasies.

"Speaking of Sereeta," Mom interjected. "Olivia and I shopped for six hours. I'm telling you, I'm not as young as I was when we went on those shopping Saturdays years ago. I am worn out."

"How'd it go with her?" Jaris asked. "She say anything about Sereeta?"

"Olivia hasn't changed much," Mom reported. "She loves to buy things whether she needs them or not. But that's not the biggest problem. She's so afraid of getting old. She's thirty-five years old, and she keeps saying her best years are behind her. She has to make every year count because the clock is ticking. She fears turning forty because then she says she'll be *really* old," Mom said sadly.

"She and that jerk she married get along any better?" Jaris asked, noticing that her mother had ignored his question about Sereeta. That worried him.

"Well," Mom responded, "I'm afraid Perry doesn't get along with Sereeta at all. He just doesn't like that poor girl. I mean, of course Sereeta doesn't like him either . . . but he's forty-four you know, Perry is. He has had a couple of relationships, but no children until Jake. He's a lot like Olivia in that he's always worrying about aging, touching up the gray in his hair, that kind of thing. I think that having a beautiful young woman like Sereeta around reminds him that he's married to a woman old enough to have a daughter who's almost an adult . . . and that bothers him."

Jaris listened closely. He hated Perry Manley already because he seemed never to have really tried to be a caring stepparent to Sereeta. He should have gone to see Sereeta in the play instead of demanding they go to a sports event. Jaris thought the man was a creep, and he wasn't even half way trying to reach out to Sereeta. Some stepfathers really made an effort. Maybe it didn't work out, but at least they made an effort.

Mom continued, the expression on her face darkening. "I think he'd like for Sereeta not to be there, Jaris," Mom figured, obviously finding it difficult to say those words.

"Not to be there?" Jaris almost yelled. "What's that mean, Mom?"

"Well, he talks about a boarding school or something for her," Mom explained.

"She's almost done with her junior year," Jaris said, the anger building up inside him, like hot lava in a volcano. "We've all gone to school together for like twelve years. We're friends. Me, Alonee, Sami, Trevor, Derrick, the whole gang of us. We've been tight since kindergarten. We grew up together in this neighborhood, and we want to be seniors together. We dreamed of being seniors together at Tubman High for all these years."

"I understand, Jaris," Mom agreed softly, her face pained. She had felt the same way when she was their age. She had grown up with a tight group of friends too. They had meant the world to her.

"Sereeta has a lot of friends who love her," Jaris protested. "We all got together and had that birthday party for her when she was feeling down. She loves her friends. It's all she's got, Mom. How could that creep think he could rip her out of where she belongs and send her to some strange school where she wouldn't know anybody? Mom, what did Sereeta's mother have to say about the idea? Is she buying it or what? Does she want to get rid of her own daughter?"

Mom frowned. "Olivia is so anxious to make this marriage work. I think she and Perry are both living a kind of fantasy. They're young kids again, starting out their married life with a baby. They wear young clothing, like teenagers do. Olivia bought most of her stuff Saturday where I take Chelsea to shop. It was so maddening. There was rock music blaring, and here we were, Olivia and I, elbowing fourteen-and fifteen-year-old girls out of the way to get to the clothing. I was embarrassed. Perry dresses like a kid too. He listens to rap music and pretends he loves it. When you see Perry from the back, you think he *is* a kid. He's slim, athletic . . . but then he turns, and here is this forty-something-year-old man and it's kinda gross. But they have this fantasy, and it's like Sereeta is disturbing the fantasy."

"So," Jaris said bitterly, "what you're saying is, she's cool with the idea of sending Sereeta away. She'd like to get rid of Sereeta, stick her in some freakin' boarding school. Is that what you're saying, Mom?"

"Yes, sweetie. I'm afraid so," Mom agreed. "Olivia will lapse into some weepy, sentimental mother thing about Sereeta, but then she's skipping through the junior's section and trying to squeeze herself into a kid's top."

"Mom, she can't do that. She can't send Sereeta away," Jaris groaned.

"What about the grandmother?" Pop said, joining the conversation. "I've met her. She's a good lady."

"She's in her seventies, though," Mom noted. "Would she want the responsibility of a teenager?"

When Jaris saw Sereeta at school, he decided not to mention the boarding school thing if she didn't. He thought she may have her own strategy for dealing with it. Instead, he said, "Sereeta, it's great that all the missing money problems have been cleared up at school, huh?"

"Yeah," Sereeta said. "It's great being in the clear!"

"So how's everything going, Sereeta?" Jaris asked nervously.

"The kids at school have sort of stopped gossiping about Mom's showing up at school like that. That's the good thing about gossip. It fades away to make a room for the next juicy bits," Sereeta half joked. "Your mom and mine went shopping the other day, huh?"

"Yeah," Jaris said.

"It's funny," Sereeta commented. "Mom wants to be younger than she is, so she dresses like a kid. I want to be older. I want to be seventeen and starting college."

Jaris didn't say anything. He was looking forward to college too. He was going to the community college about three miles away. Then he'd transfer to the state university and take the education units he needed to be a teacher. Most of Jaris's friends were doing the same thing, so the little gang from Tubman would be together. Except for Sereeta, Jaris thought painfully.

"They'd like me to move out right now and go to boarding school," Sereeta stated in a calm voice. "They can't wait for college."

"Your mom wants that?" Jaris asked in a shaken voice. He knew about it, of course, but he had been hoping that his mother may have made too much of Olivia's comments. Jaris had hoped that Sereeta's mother really didn't want her sixteen-year-old girl to move away.

"Well, Perry wants it, and whatever Perry wants, Perry gets," Sereeta explained. "We don't get along, you know, my stepfather and me. We don't fight or anything. We just quietly hate each other. Maybe 'hate' is too strong a word. He doesn't like me and I don't like him. And the funny part is, neither one of us is really to blame. I don't like him because he's not my father and because Mom cares more for him than she does for me. He dislikes me because I remind him that he's not a kid anymore. His wife is poking at her face, and putting on antiwrinkle cream, and talking about getting a little nip and tuck eventually. But how young can she be with a kid my age? It's like we'd both like the other one to disappear. But I don't know how to make him disappear, and he thinks he's found a way to make me disappear."

"Sereeta," Jaris begged her in an impassioned voice, "you can't let them send you to boarding school. They can't make you go. The school wouldn't want a student who hated being there. You know how we've all planned to do our senior year together at Tubman. We're almost there, Sereeta. She can't take that away from us."

"I know, Jaris," Sereeta agreed. "But we—me and Perry—can be like two scorpions in a bottle, ripping at each other in that hateful house that isn't home anymore. The war will just continue."

"Sereeta, so many kids are your friends at Tubman. We're a team. Remember your birthday party? We all love you so much . . . I, uh, love you in a special way, but you've got a lotta real friends . . . please, Sereeta, don't let anybody do this to you—to us."

Sereeta smiled. She leaned forward and kissed Jaris on the lips. "I love you too. Didn't I tell you that when you gave me those magnificent earrings? But I feel sorry for you, Jaris, loving somebody like me. I am so not like you. You got it all together, and I'm flying off the planet in a million little pieces."

"Like a broken doll," Jaris thought but didn't say the words. Instead, he kept trying to change her mind.

"That's not my doing," Jaris told her. "My parents are solid, and you got a different kind of family. A few times when my parents were arguing, I almost panicked. I thought how could I deal with them splitting up? I felt like I was in an earth-quake and the ground was shaking. I hate change when it means losing people I care about."

"I guess change is part of life, or so they say," Sereeta mused.

"But not now, Sereeta," Jaris persisted. "Not for you and me. Not you being pulled out of Tubman when you need to be there, when you belong there. After we graduate from Tubman, I hope we're still close when we go to college, but I'm not talking about that now. I want you in my senior year at Tubman, Sereeta. If you're not there, then I don't care about anything, I swear. I don't even care if I go to freakin' high school or if I drop out and become a motorcycle bum."

Sereeta laughed a forlorn little laugh. "Now you got me scared, Jaris. You're get-ting to be a crazy person like me. Maybe we're more alike than I thought."

CHAPTER TEN

Ms. McDowell scheduled the first of the three rehearsals for the Tubman birthday celebration in the school auditorium. The teacher was in jeans and a black pullover, and she looked stunning as she came on stage and addressed the students working on the program.

"We've created really great scenery," she began, "thanks to some amazing students. The background is going to look like a gloomy, woodsy area in the South where Tubman led her little band of fugitive slaves. Destini Fletcher and Trevor Jenkins painted the scenes and designed the background, and to them a humble thank-you. We've got excellent lighting, and the glee club has promised to outdo themselves. But the focus is going to be on you guys, the actors. You all have good voices, and you need to put your heart into this."

Ms. McDowell smiled encouragingly to all the students and then nodded to Marko Lane. Marko stepped on stage and flashed a proud smile. Like the others, he was already in costume dressed in a ragged white shirt and dark trousers. "I can't imagine bein' a slave," Marko announced. "Anybody trying to make me a slave would have his head busted first."

"All right, Marko," Ms. McDowell said impatiently. "We all know you're a proud, strong young man who treasures his freedom and wouldn't tolerate slavery. But that's easy for us to say because we were born free, unlike our African-American ancestors. My own great grandmother was a slave in Louisiana. So just do your part, Marko."

Marko stood there and held forth: "My name is Benjamin and I am twenty-eight years old. I have suffered under slavery all my life. My back bears the scars of many a whippin'. I don't remember my mother or father. My mistress was a devilish woman who showed us no mercy. Then one night this lady showed me the way to freedom. Along came Harriett Tubman."

Alonee got up to read. She was playing a slave named Jane, owned by the worst man in the county and beaten daily. Derrick Shaw and Kevin Walker read their parts with strong emotion.

Then it was Jaris's turn. He had been looking forward to making his presentation, but now his heart was heavy with worry over Sereeta's future. That anxiety cast a dark shadow over everything. Still, he gave it his best.

"My name is Charles Nalle. I escaped slavery and made it all the way to Troy, New York, where there was no slavery. I thought I was safe, but the slave catchers tracked me down. Even in a free state, I was not free. They dragged me off to return me to my master in the South. But suddenly a woman came out of nowhere. She grabbed the officer holding me and pushed him away. The she wrapped her arms around me and cried, 'Don't let them have him,' and I was saved. She was Harriett Tubman."

Finally it was time for Sereeta. Jaris looked at the slim, fragile girl. He wanted to put his arms around her as Harriet Tubman had put her arms around that young slave. Jaris wanted to save Sereeta, but he didn't know how.

Sereeta briefly recited the life of Harriet Tubman, speaking in the first person. She told of her harrowing childhood, the struggles of her adult life, and the courage to lead so many fugitive slaves to freedom. In a faltering voice, Sereeta described the moment of freedom, "The sun came up and shimmered like gold through the trees."

Ms. McDowell was pleased with the first dress rehearsal. "It's going to be excellent," she announced. "I'm proud of all of you."

After the rehearsal, Pop picked Sereeta and Jaris up for the ride home.

"Coming to see us celebrate Harriet Tubman's birthday in two weeks, Mr. Spain?" Sereeta asked.

"Girl, you better believe it," Pop replied. "Monie and I'll be there for you both. I'm really looking forward to it. What a great idea. I mean, everybody knows the name of the school and that Tubman was a great lady. But how many kids or parents really got the lowdown on that amazing woman? They don't know from nothing about her. They got all the sports stats for these jerks hauling in a million bucks a season or more. They know who's splitting with who in Hollywood. But we don't know much about the people who made this country great. It's a rotten shame."

He glanced at Sereeta. "We'll be there to see our boy, Jaris, and you too, baby girl. Harriet Tubman is somewhere in a golden place, and she's looking over the whole situation. I know she's mighty proud of the girl who gets to play her."

"Thank you," Sereeta responded, her voice trembling a little. Jaris could see she was deeply touched by the compliment.

Jaris spent hours wondering how he might change what was about to happen to Sereeta. He felt he had at least to try to talk some sense into her mother and stepfather. He knew it was not his place to get involved and they'd probably resent it. Even Sereeta wouldn't want it, Jaris thought. But he had to try. So, when Sereeta went over to visit her grandmother on a Thursday night before a school holiday and said she'd be gone until Friday afternoon, Jaris made his move. He rode his motorcycle over to the Manley house.

Jaris rapped on the door and Perry Manley appeared. "Hi Mr. Manley. I'm Jaris Spain—I'm—" he began.

"Yes, I know who you are. You're her boyfriend," Mr. Manley said with a noticeable lack of warmth.

"I was wondering if I could come in and talk to you and your wife for just a few minutes," Jaris asked. His voice was cracking. His knees were knocking together so badly he hoped Manley couldn't hear them. He thought to himself, "You fool, what makes you think you can change the minds of these adults—you, a sixteen-year-old jerk!"

But he had to try.

"Come in," Manley said. "We have a dinner engagement in about forty-five minutes, but if you can be brief." Then he called to another room, "Olivia, there's a boy here, a friend of Sereeta's. He wants to talk to us."

Olivia came into the room as Jaris sat down in the living room. She had finally remembered Jaris's name. "Hello Jaris," she said with a wan smile. "So nice to see you again."

"I bet you guys are excited that Sereeta was chosen to play Harriet Tubman in the birthday celebration at Tubman High, huh?" Jaris started. "It's quite an honor."

"Oh?" Manley replied. "She hasn't told us yet."

"I think she mentioned something about it, sweetheart," Mrs. Manley remarked in a timid voice.

"Uh, what I came to ask you guys . . . ," Jaris began, "Sereeta said something about maybe doing her senior year at a boarding school and not finishing at Tubman. I just wanted you to know she's got so many friends at Tubman and they love her a lot. I think, you know, she needs the support of her friends for her senior year. We've all been together for like twelve years and graduating together has always been a big dream for all of us." Jaris got his message out, in spite of the thunderous pounding of his heart.

"Well, we have to consider what's best for her," Manley responded. He looked at his watch, then continued. "She's been under a lot of stress adjusting to things, and we thought it might be best for her to be in an entirely new environment. She might be better able to put her problems behind her."

"Yes," Sereeta's mother agreed. "The poor child has tried to adjust, but she has her issues."

Jaris grew desperate and, in his desperation, had to speak up. "Sereeta has had a hard time with the family situation here. She thinks she doesn't count for much around here. So if you separate her from her friends too, then she has nobody, you know?"

"Doesn't count for much?" Manley snapped. "How absurd! My wife and I have moved heaven and earth to try to help that girl accept me. She is a bitter young woman who has refused to accept that my wife and I married. She can be quite hateful at times, and she is creating intolerable problems for us."

Olivia Manley dabbed at her eyes with the corner of a lace handkerchief. "We've tried," she whimpered. "But Sereeta does not seem to care about my happiness, only her own."

"Young man," Mr. Manley asserted, "I'm sure you had the best of intentions when you came here, but the truth is, this is not your business. You are Sereeta's teenaged boyfriend, not her family. I'm sure you will have many other girlfriends. You don't want to lose your current girl-friend. The social lives of people your age are constantly changing, but we have much more important concerns. We have to pro-tect our home and our marriage. We have to build a home for our son. Sereeta, quite frankly, does not belong here. She is not happy here, and she is making us unhappy. That is the way it is." Mr. Manley looked at his watch again and got up. He expected that to be a signal for Jaris to leave. Olivia Manley was now weeping softly.

"So you're throwing her out, right?" Jaris asked bitterly. "Like the old curtains that don't match your new sofa."

"How ugly of you to put it that way," Mr. Manley declared. "You are a rude young man, and I don't like you very much. We are sending her to a boarding school for her own good and for the good of this family."

"You never cared about her," Jaris told her, anger and sorrow rising inside him. "You didn't even go see her when she played in *A Tale of Two Cities*. She was the female lead! All the parents came. But you didn't. She was so hurt. You should've seen her crying about that."

"Good evening to you, young man, and do not come again," Perry Manley commanded. "You are not welcome."

As Jaris got up and turned to go, Olivia Manley looked up at him and sobbed. "J-Jaris, I do care. I *do* care. Ohhh, as God is my judge, I do care . . . but I . . . I . . . don't know how to love her. I don't know how to love her anymore." She lowered her face into her hands and wept as Jaris left the house. Jaris knew he had failed miserably in what he had come to do. Sereeta may even be furious that he had come.

But he had to try.

Sereeta never said anything to Jaris about his visit to her house, and Jaris didn't bring it up. He didn't know if she knew he'd come, and he wouldn't try to find out.

A few weeks later, a large crowd of people gathered at the high school on the night of the Harriet Tubman birthday celebration. Parents and friends of the students quickly filled the auditorium seats. People from the media—from the newspapers and television stations—had come to cover the unusual event. Schools didn't usually have birthday parties for their namesakes, especially when no one was even sure of the person's exact birthday.

Jaris's parents came early. They waved at him as he got ready to take his place. They were in a front row. Jaris's grandmother, his mother's mother, whom Jaris did not even like much, came as well. Jaris recognized all his friends' parents.

Jaris did not see Perry and Olivia Manley in the auditorium, but maybe they would still show up. They might be latecomers. Jaris had told them how hurt Sereeta was that they hadn't seen her in *A Tale of Two Cities*. So maybe they would come to this. Jaris clung to a fantasy that even he did not believe—a warm moment between Sereeta, her mother, and stepfather. He dreamed of an unlikely healing, like those in tearjerker movies as the music swelled.

The curtain opened with the glee club singing old spirituals. The ringing lyrics of "Go Down, Moses" and "Let My People Go" filled the auditorium. Then the dramatic scenery was exposed, and the players walked out, one by one, each lit by a stark spotlight. Jaris had to admit that Marko Lane looked and sounded great. He spoke with throbbing emotion in his strong tenor voice.

The sound effects of groaning and clanking chains accompanied the stories of the other slaves. Alonee, Kevin, and Derrick all looked and sounded powerful. And then it was time for Sereeta.

Sereeta wore a long gray dress, and she looked small and haggard on the stage. But she still looked beautiful, because not even the drab dress and the shabby surroundings could dull her sparkling eyes or diminish the loveliness of her dark curls against the honey brown skin of her face. She stood still and erect at midstage, illuminated by a single spotlight, and spoke.

"I am Harriet Tubman," she began in a strong voice. "I was born around 1820 and I grew up a slave. Until I was about five, I played in the woods with other children. But when I was six I was put to work. When I didn't do a good job of cleaning the house, I was whipped. One day, when I was fifteen, I helped a boy escape slavery. An overseer was so angry he threw a lead weight at me. It hit me in the head, and it left a dent in my forehead for the rest of my life. I suffered bad headaches and often I fainted. When I was in my twenties, I ran from my slave master, and then I helped many others escape North into Canada. They called me the Black Moses because I led my people to freedom. I will never forget the first day

I was free. 'There was such glory over everything . . . ' "

Tears shone on Sereeta's cheeks. "I am Harriet Tubman . . . nothing could stop me. Cruel masters could not stop me. Poverty could not stop me. The pain and suffering of my life could not stop me. I overcame it all. You can too. We all can . . . no matter what pain or sorrow comes into your lives you can overcome as I did . . . I am Harriet Tubman and I saw the light."

The glee club broke into the civil rights anthem, "We Shall Overcome," to the thunderous applause of the audience. Everybody shouted, "Happy birthday, Harriet Tubman!"

Backstage, behind the curtain, the cast hugged and congratulated one another before changing their clothes. Afterward, Ms. McDowell told them all they were great and dismissed them. Jaris saw Sereeta and asked, "Want a ride home, babe?"

Sereeta smiled at him, took him by the hand to midstage, and pulled the curtain aside enough for them to look out. They poked their heads out from behind the curtain. The audience had left the auditorium, but one elderly lady sat there in a purple dress. She had honey brown skin and sparkling eyes. She saw Sereeta, waved to her, and winked.

Back behind the curtain, Sereeta told Jaris, "I'm going home with Grandma . . . for good."

Jaris hugged Sereeta with all his might. It was so good to see her laughing at last—his little doll.